New Bad News

SARABANDE BOOKS
Louisville, KY

NEW

RYAN RIDGE

BAD

STORIES

NEWS

Library of Congress Cataloging-in-Publication Data

Names: Ridge, Ryan, 1978.
Title: New bad news / Ryan Ridge.
Description: First edition. | Louisville, KY : Sarabande Books, 2020.
Identifiers: LCCN 2019032536 | ISBN 9781946448569 (trade paperback)
ISBN 9781946448576 (e-book)
Subjects: LCSH: Hollywood (Los Angeles, Calif.)—Fiction.
Flash fiction, American. | Short stories, American.
Hollywood (Los Angeles, Calif.)—Poetry. | Prose poems, American.
Short stories, American.
Classification: LCC PS3618.I3916 A6 2020
DDC 813/.6—dc23
LC record available at https://lccn.loc.gov/2019032536

Cover and interior design by Alban Fischer.
Manufactured in Canada.
This book is printed on acid-free paper.
Sarabande Books is a nonprofit literary organization.

This project is supported in part by an award from the
National Endowment for the Arts. The Kentucky Arts Council,
the state arts agency, supports Sarabande Books with state tax dollars
and federal funding from the National Endowment for the Arts.

In memory of my father, John,
who loved long shots
and underdogs.

You know that the best you can expect is to avoid the worst.

—ITALO CALVINO, *If on a Winter's Night a Traveler*

Contents

Echo Park

Jackson Browne

I grew up reading Shakespeare and Mark Twain.

—JACKSON BROWNE

These days he strums his guitar with an unregistered handgun in an alleyway at the Psychedelic Street Fair. The acoustics are astonishing. After the failure of the '60s came the disappointment of the '70s. Now every decade feels like the last. It's a story older than prime real estate itself. In the Country Western sunshine, our heartbeats beat in three-four time as you waltz into an Albertsons on Alvarado to buy a bag of avocados. Everything costs more in California. Nothing is sacred but profitable cinema. Out-of-work actors can't catch a break, so, instead, we fall into afternoon movies: comedy, dramedy, urban tragedy. Most lives are silent films no one sees. He handguns his guitar in an alleyway at the Psychedelic Street Fair. His weapons of choice are: (1) his voice and (2) an acoustic piano dropped from a ballroom balcony in the rain, but it rarely ever rains anymore. These minor chords sound exactly like the distance between us. And the ocean? It belongs only to itself.

Diary

We were living hard, but it was hardly living. Some of the skinniest skin stars claimed they fasted to enhance their five-figure salaries while the fairest among us airbrushed ourselves to death. These were the new industry standards, which—even by our standards—were low. And we knew that most of the flyover demographic would be appalled by the ways we partied in the California moonlight night after night, but we did it anyway. I mean, freedom isn't free, right? Entertainment and war are our only exports anymore. Once, a bald eagle landed on the Paramount lot, and all the actors saluted, and the crew members shouted their support for the troops and for once, just once, we felt like we were winning. Later, we heard drum machines and shamans in the distance, and we did what any young aspiring artists would: we ate more magic mushrooms and charged everything to our credit cards and asked questions after. My life felt like a commercial break before it broke. I used small bills as coke straws to stay in touch with my modest origins. Like my mentor, Harry Dean Stanton, I left Kentucky and to Kentucky I hope never to return. If I'm lucky, really lucky, they'll name a burning building or a car crash after me.

Fire Consumes Businesses
near the Freeway

Fire consumes businesses near the freeway the first Friday of every third month. The sign above tonight's burning building says: NEED CASH NOW. But with the sign on fire, it's no longer a sign: it's a smoldering metaphor. Education is not the filling of a pail, but the lighting of a fire (Yeats). The residents have gathered together this evening to watch the blaze. They swallow edible marijuana and share stories from the golden days of television. There's no business like unemployment. From our vantage point, the fiery sign says: - - - - - ASH NOW. To me, there's nothing wrong with this as a business model.

Modern Times

*I was determined to continue making silent films, ... I was a pantomimist
and in that medium I was unique and, without false modesty, a master.*

—CHARLIE CHAPLIN

Stop me if you've heard this one before: I met an aspiring comedian from Minneapolis at the dispensary. In the lobby, she showed me her half-ironic Charlie Chaplin tattoo. It was a tramp stamp at the base of her spine featuring the Little Tramp's face. We were intimate that night in her studio apartment in Studio City. The entire deal occurred in silence "in honor of Charlie's legacy." That's what she said. The lights were on, and we were high on edible sativa. The mood had caught up with us, and I was behind her, looking down at Chaplin's face looking up at me. Afterward, I felt a strange kinship with all his films. Although I never saw the comedian or her tattoo again, I've seen *Modern Times* at least a dozen times now.

Babe Ruth's Bachelor Pad

Whatever it was it wasn't enough. Millions admired him, and it wasn't enough. Enough was enough. He was blackout drunk again at the Crown Hill Apartments in South Echo Park where he maintained an off-season bachelor pad despite the disapproval of his estranged wife, Helen, in New York City. In those days, he hit 370 for the Yankees and otherwise hit on anything that moved. Tonight, he had a couple of beauties with him, starlets of the silent screen. The blonde sat on one knee, and the brunette sat on the other. They poured a bottle of champagne on his head and then used the champagne as the lubricant for a scalp massage. Now he felt clean, and after that, once the girls were gone, he called his estranged wife in New York City. But she didn't answer, and he hung up and called his shot. He pointed at the bed, and his head hit the pillow like a walk-off grand slam. That night he dreamed about his orphaned childhood. Otherwise, he dreamed of oblivion.

The News

Tonight, my doctor calls like a doctor in a bad joke and says he has some good news and some bad news and which do I want first. "Let's go with the good," I say. "Sure," he says. "The good news is that your wife is fine." I say, "My wife?" He says, "Correct." I say, "Okay, what's up with her?" "Well," he says, "she's sick. Sick of it all." I say, "Can you please put it in layman's terms, doc?" "Yes," he says. "She's tired of her job, her marriage, and the children she never had on account of a career that never materialized. What I find best in a scenario such as this is to take a little time off and get away. Now, I'm going to be golfing on Maui tomorrow, and I've invited her to tag along." I say, "You've invited her to tag along?" "Yes," he says. "She's quite athletic, and I think that she'll make an excellent addition to our threesome." "I see," I say. He says, "Now are you ready for the bad news?" I say, "Lay it on me." "Unfortunately," he says, "this procedure isn't covered under insurance." "That's absurd," I say. "This is why we need health-care reform immediately." He says, "You're preaching to the choir!" I say, "What are they singing?" He says, "'Doctor My Eyes' by Jackson Browne." I say, "I love that song." He says, "That makes two of us." "Doctor," I say, "there's just one thing." "What is it?" he says. I say, "I don't have a wife anymore, haven't for some time now. Last I heard, she's shacking up with a Netflix exec up by the Bay." "Well," he says, "I don't suppose you have his number? She refuses to answer her cell." "No," I say. "Sorry." Two weeks later, I got a bill in the mail for our conversation. He was an excellent doctor: the best in LA County.

Pilots

On the rooftop of a Hollywood hotel, the tourists eye the other tourists by the peanut-shaped pool. They're getting rheumy-eyed on rum and oiling themselves down in the sun, reading paperbacks with semierotic titles like *Alice in Chains Again* and *Cupids on Jet Skis*. One woman whistles for the bartender. That's me. Her drink isn't going to refill itself. Her small son hunts insects in the faux grass with a magnifying glass. Our lifeguard is a licensed realtor, sells luxury condos and lofts overlooking other luxury condos and lofts. I'm thinking of buying if this new pilot gets picked up. Now the little boy sees something beneath the magnifying glass and motions for me to look. Below the lens, a gigantic ant is being immolated in the August sunlight. The ant's antennae are smoking, and this idiotic kid is laughing. I deliver his mother her drink. "Great son you've got there," I say. "He's a complete psychopath," she says. "The world's smallest CEO. He takes after his father. Rub some lotion on my back?" I oblige. "Thank you," she says afterward. "Don't mention it," I say. "It's my job. But not my real job." She lowers her sunglasses. "I'm an actor," I say. "I don't think I've ever seen you in anything," she says. "No, I remember faces and I don't remember yours." "I've mostly done pilots," I say. "Pilots," she says. "I've done a few of those, too."

Neighbors

My neighbor, the librarian, throws quiet parties on the weekends. Word is she's an avid speed-reader. She and her colleagues get cranked up on Adderall and speed through *Infinite Jest* in a night. The next day they play parlor games on the dead lawn, charading into the evening as I admire them from my panoptical balcony window. They are undoubtedly decent people, despite conflicting reports in the neighborhood newsletters. You can tell by the PG-13 placement of their hands as they slow dance in the climax of a California sunset that these are the kind of people you wouldn't mind living next door to. I mean if they invited you to a party, you would go. I would.

I Guess I Soured

We met on the set of a vegan bacon commercial, then went whole hog and took a cruise around Catalina Island. Saw nothing but fog. We pondered the fourth dimension while driving in fifth gear along the coast. I guess I soured when I heard she'd married a craft beer distributor. The keys jingled in my windbreaker pocket as I walked away. Back in my Echo Park apartment, I got higher than God's zipper on dispensary dope and cataloged my failures on Post-it Notes. Through the cheap walls, I heard expensive laughter. I felt sad about something I couldn't quite place.

Elliott Smith

Once he was outside of time. He was almost dead. An accident, an overdose, an accidental overdose. When his heart stopped, he saw a range of light—the full vivid spectrum, which briefly formed a baby rainbow on the *Figure 8* wall on Sunset. He passed through a door and entered the studio. On the other side, he found himself in a near-dark conference room. There was a projector on one wall and across the table was a screen. He sat down, and a documentary began playing. It was a film called *Mr. Misery*. In it, everything that had ever happened in his life was happening at once, and it was too much. He said, "Stop! Stop! Stop!" And it stopped. Then he was in a hospital bed, and the nurse said, "We thought we lost you." He said, "I have déjà vu." She said, "Just relax." He said, "I don't know how. Do you?" She said, "I don't understand the question." Afterward, he questioned everything. The nurse handed him his guitar and a nitrous balloon. Between chords, you could hear someone coughing in an adjacent room. The next day was the next week, and he was dead in a bungalow in Echo Park, a knife in his chest, which his lover removed. "Maybe his suicide was a homicide? Maybe his misery was finally too much?" Again he is outside of time—deader than someone who's dead wrong—his spirit spilled onto wax forever.

The Wax Museum

I rode my Triumph up to the Hollywood Wax Museum. I paid the ticket person and stood in front of the Terminator statue for a long time. I was so high I convinced the statue I was real. The Terminator lunged at me when I reached to touch his cheek and next thing I know I'm in a headlock and he says: "I need your clothes, your boots, and your motorcycle." It turns out that the statue was Arnold Schwarzenegger in disguise. He was out doing some promo spots for the latest release. There's footage of it on the internet. People tell me it's hilarious, but that's not the way it felt at the time. No, that afternoon, when the Terminator had me in a headlock, I was certain that the uncanny had become sentient and was intent on destroying humanity, starting with me. I haven't gone near the Wax Museum since, but now I have Arnold's autograph on the side of my motorcycle helmet. "Hasta la vista, baby," I sometimes think as I drive away from people, trying to look fearless.

A Place beyond That Place

When she opens her legs, I listen. Best skip it and go to the afterglow. Oh, it was such stupid math, that afternoon, in her blue bedroom. Somehow a sister was involved. A landlord, too. I left. There is a place up the road, past Alvarado. I see a woman there sometimes. She collects animals in her home, dead animals—stuffed and exotic. That woman and those animals, they follow you with their eyes. There's something between us that isn't love. It's much worse. I drive past her animal palace tonight. I'm on the Triumph with the headlights off, because there is a place beyond that place if you keep going. It is a place where the lights inside have dimmed forever.

Postal

In a long line at the PO on Alvarado, and the dude in front of me turns around and yawns in my face. "This place is the worst," he says, tilting his head like someone cheating at pinball. "Do you see that albino woman in front of us with prosthetic legs?" "No," I say, glancing at a big guy in a little fedora. "Good," he says. "Because there is no albino woman with prosthetic legs. I made that up. It was a test. I wanted to make sure you weren't crazy because I was talking to a guy in line at the DMV the other day and he was crazy. You know what he said to me?" "No idea," I say. "The guy looked at me," he says. "He looked me straight in the eyes and told me he was my father. You believe that?" "Was he?" I say. "My father," he says, "was killed in a drunk-driving accident twenty years ago. It was his fault. He got shit-faced and flipped a golf cart on himself. Besides, I hated the bastard. When I'm through mailing this package, I'll head over to Hollywood Forever and dance on his grave. Care to join me?" "Look, man," I say, "if you're hitting on me, I'm flattered but not interested." "Hitting on you," he says, "please. I'm into tulips. Two lips here," he says pointing to his mouth, "and two lips here," he says pointing at his crotch. "That's four lips altogether," I say. "Bingo," he says. Just then, an albino woman with prosthetic legs rolls into the PO on a motorized scooter. She's wearing nothing but a boa constrictor. I blink my eyes, and she's still there. Again: again. "Do you see that albino woman with prosthetic legs?" I ask the man in front of me. "No," he says. "I am your father," I say. "Let's go and slow dance on my grave."

If I Were a Thoroughbred

Flashback: Something shattered, and Dad said, "Old age and treachery always slay innocence and optimism." I said, "How do we even exist in this negative-energy dimension?" He had no answers. I spent much of my youth faking leg injuries to skip out on track practice. If I were a thoroughbred, I'd have been put down.

Location

You are not paralyzed on beer by a diminishing river. You are not setting the doghouse on fire on the lawn. You are not banking in Zurich or London or any of the secret tax shelters of the Caribbean. You are not camping under a bridge downtown or beneath any of the great expressway ramps in the suburbs. You are not getting high on the roof of the hospital with a rowdy orderly named Ronnie. You are not dancing with yourself at your best friend's second wedding. You are not developing a film in an undeveloped country. You are not returning to school to become an X-ray technician. You are not breaking down on an LA freeway on your way to a Silver Lake potluck. You are not drinking port wine with the longshoremen in San Pedro again. You are not stealing Roberto Bolaño books from the nearby library. You are not posing for the spy satellites at a teenage riot. You are not riding your Triumph straight into the sea. You are here. You are still here.

Echo Park

In the 1880s, when the workers were building the reservoir for the human-made lake, you could hear their voices echoing off the canyon walls. "It sounds like a park of echoes," someone remarked. "An echo park," someone else said, and it stuck. And it stuck. And it stuck.

Echoes of Echo Park

American Apparel apparel, American Apparel apparel, American Apparel apparel . . . beard, beard, beard . . . coffee shop, coffee shop, coffee shop . . . dive bar, dive bar, dive bar . . . Etsy design, Etsy design, Etsy design . . . fixed gear, fixed gear, fixed gear . . . glasses (extra-thick), glasses (extra-thick), glasses (extra-thick) . . . headphones, headphones, headphones . . . irony, irony, irony . . . judgment, judgment, judgment . . . kombucha, kombucha, kombucha . . . lifestyle brand, lifestyle brand, lifestyle brand . . . millennial, millennial, millennial . . . novelist, novelist, novelist . . . owl tattoo, owl tattoo, owl tattoo . . . PBR, PBR, PBR . . . quilter, quilter, quilter . . . Ray-Bans, Ray-Bans, Ray-Bans . . . screenwriter, screenwriter, screenwriter . . . typewriter, typewriter, typewriter . . . undercut, undercut, undercut . . . vinyl, vinyl, vinyl . . . witty banter, witty banter, witty banter . . . Gen X, Gen X, Gen X . . . YOLO, YOLO, YOLO . . . zombie, zombie, zombie . . .

All of us. All of us. All of us.

Church

The gangs have gone away, priced out to Eagle Rock, El Sereno, and the innards of the Inland Empire. On weekends, they return to their home turf in old Mercurys and souped-up pickups. They do this as a way of reconnecting with their roots. And if it's true what they say about place giving rise to spirit, then the spirit of Echo Park is positively Western in a cinematic sense. Most Saturday nights culminate in a gunfight. Tonight shots ring out on Preston Avenue and echo on up to Avalon. Now an aspiring gangster is dead in a stairwell on Armitage. Tomorrow, I will step under police tape on my way to church. My church is called the Gold Room on Sunset. This is back when you could still get a PBR and a shot of tequila for four bucks. The peanuts? Free. I will sit at the end of the bar, drinking and praying for work. I won't be able to tell if the drinking enhances the praying or if the praying improves the drink. Amen. Lord, hear our prayer.

Coyote

Night calls the animals to the streets. I'm on the Triumph shifting gears amid my own shiftlessness. At the corner of Mohawk and Reservoir, a scrawny coyote sifts through the contents of a trash can. In neighborhood newsletter editorials, coyotes are nuisances. In folklore, they are trickster figures—whenever one shows up, watch out: something exciting is about to happen. I'm stopped at a traffic light, watching the coyote lap up leftover malt liquor from a forty of Colt 45. I admire a coyote that drinks. I give my horn a quick tap of approval. The coyote looks at me with its eyes aglow. I look at the coyote. And for a split second we understand all there is to understand; we understand each other. Nothing lasts. The light changes.

Noir

There's the slant of the shoreline and the lights of the oil derricks reflecting off the black water like a miniature city, and when the detective arrives to make the cash drop at the dark edge of the pier he's struck by two things at once: (1) the vast existential loneliness of LA at night, and (2) a blackjack to the back of the head.

The Second Detective

Have I mentioned the cam girl? She was not a girl at all: a woman, an artist. What I mean is she had a job that ran counter to her passion. The detective signed into the chatroom and scanned the comments in the right-hand column: men—assholes, virgins more than likely—were making demands. The scene reminded him of an amateur hostage negotiation. He lit a cigar, sipped his scotch, watched the artist pull her panties to the side and push the vibrator close. Now the detective sat back and blew a smoke ring. The artist closed her eyes. He swallowed his scotch hard, felt like crying. Instead, he typed: "This is no longer a missing person's case. I'll notify your family." It'd been two years since they'd seen her. The family? They were from a Midwestern state that was all vowels and had no idea what was being broadcast from California bedrooms. "Tell them I said hello," she typed back. "Tell them we all do what we have to do to live in this world. The dead would kill to live." The detective didn't argue. He extinguished his cigar. Case closed. The only reason I know any of this is because the detective told me the tale one afternoon at the Gold Room. Later, the detective disappeared, too. His family hired a private investigator to look into it, and, one afternoon, the detective's investigator knocked on my door. I told him the story about the detective telling me about finding the missing girl online. The second detective didn't think there was much to it, but he thanked me for my time.

Last Cigarette

"Every cigarette you don't smoke adds another four-point-eight minutes to your life," a concerned citizen said to me one afternoon in front of Paramount Pictures after I botched an audition. I did not light my cigarette. I left. Five minutes later, I stood at the Hollywood Forever Cemetery torching a Lucky Strike in front of Rudolph Valentino's mausoleum. Now that guy liked his cigarettes. I was picturing him smoking in one of those old silent pictures when some punk kid interrupted my fun. The blood-red lettering on his T-shirt said: PUNK'S STILL DEAD. "Hey, man," the kid said, "where's Johnny Ramone?" I told him Johnny Ramone was in heaven now. "No shit, shitbird," he said. "I'm looking for his stone." I lit another cigarette. The kid made an outrageous face and said, "You shouldn't do that." I exhaled, said, "What?" "Your selfish, nihilistic attitude toward your own health is not only destroying you and the planet," he said, "but it's also exposing me to harmful toxins, and, because I'd like to grow up to be a successful entertainment attorney, I can't have that. Either put out that cigarette or face the consequences." I took another drag, and he pulled out a switchblade and stuck me in the stomach. I sat down on the side of the mausoleum, bleeding. The kid vanished behind a nearby tomb. I finished my cigarette.

Red Hill

Before WWII there were so many socialists living in the foothills of Echo Park that the locals referred to it as Red Hill. The place was a haven for druggies and radicals, witches and freaks. Woody Guthrie even lived there for a spell. Yes, Echo Park was an Eden unto its own. Then came the Red Scare, the Lavender Scare, and the Everyone-Is-Scared-of-Everyone-Else Scare. Names were named. Careers ruined. Lives wrecked. All for what? Ideas? "No ideas but in things," said William Carlos Williams. Williams was blacklisted for a poem called *The Pink Church*. Everyone assumed the poem was about communism because it had the word "pink" in the title. I, too, flirted with communism when I first moved to Echo Park. Most days I walked around in a Che Guevara T-shirt and a beret. Then one night I got stomped outside the Griffith Observatory by a couple of coked-up bikers and thought worse of things. I had the fear, or the fear had me. Next month I bought the Triumph, a closet full of Western shirts, and a pistol. Day after, I bought another pistol and shot the original pistol and then took the Triumph up to Pasadena and tossed both pistols off the Colorado Street Bridge.

Adjuncts

It was teacher appreciation night at the wine bar, and, although they weren't appreciated much in the larger pyramid scheme of the contemporary, corporate education model, the adjuncts drank for half off on Monday nights during the school year, and they drank double. I drank with them. I wasn't an adjunct. I was an actor between roles, which meant I tended bar at a rooftop hotel in Hollywood and drove rich guys to LAX in a secret cab service that catered to execs and daytime television actors off the Fox lot. Sometimes the execs wanted handjobs, and, if the price was right, I offered them a hand. I was also adapting a Roberto Bolaño novel into a screenplay. The adjuncts spent their days in classrooms and their evenings on various interstates. They were freeway fliers, scholars, and creative types: PhDs and MFAs who lived in Echo Park but taught in out-of-the-way places like Irvine, Fullerton, Long Beach, and Northridge. After a long day of shaping the minds of the future for minimum wage, they needed strong, cheap drinks and casual conversation. It was an eclectic crew: gay, trans, straight; you name it. I loved the way they spoke in such reverent tones about their prospects for tenure-track jobs, book deals, and lucrative freelance gigs. It reminded me of the way fellow actors talked about TV pilots and attributed movie work. That was what I had in common with these adjunct professors: we were all waiting for our lives to start. I'd step outside with my e-cigarette and check my iPhone to see if my agent had called. Mostly she had not. I'd take slow drags and exhale slower, watching the sunset die behind a row of palms.

Unemployment Office

My screenplay wasn't working so I sent it to the unemployment office.

Extras

They give you fifty bucks a day to be an extra in the studio audience. The only prerequisite is that you are alive. I was broke and in need of cash fast, which meant I was in the studio audience up in Century City for one of the few shows which still used studio audiences. It was a sitcom I'd previously auditioned for. I'd come close to getting one of the leads, but they'd gone in "a different direction." Now the character I would've played was declaiming brilliant life advice to his adopted daughter after she was booed off the stage at her student talent show. It was one of those heartfelt moments where the audience says *Awww* and claps, but I couldn't contain myself: I was laughing, but it wasn't funny. And I was causing my own scene because I was supposed to be clapping. I got up to leave. The man in the aisle seat glanced awkwardly at my crotch as I passed. "Excuse me," I said. "Sorry." They'd still mail me fifty bucks. I passed a line of extras waiting in the sun. Like most days, more had shown up than they needed.

Island Time

They filmed the television show *Gilligan's Island* on a soundstage in Echo Park. Years later, I watched the entire series on DVD in my Echo Park apartment, a couple of blocks from where the soundstage had been. I wasn't working much, aside from an occasional commercial spot. I had plenty of time to drink and not think and binge old TV. *Gilligan's Island* was my favorite. I'd get deep into gin and watch a dozen episodes in a row. Island Time, I called it. What I admired most about the show was the total lack of continuity between episodes. Zero story memory. It was as if each day was the first day on the island for old Gilligan and company, which was precisely the way my life felt: purgatoried in some zany twilight zone. I also watched a lot of *Twilight Zone*.

Echo Parking Meters

Certain side stories were running concurrently: (1) Time had expired forever for the old Echo Park parking meters, and now they'd replaced the traditional meters with automated pay stations, which accepted credit cards and payment via cell phones. (2) It was May, which meant they were screening night movies at the Hollywood Forever Cemetery. *Cool Hand Luke* played on the side of Rudolph Valentino's mausoleum, and Paul Newman was cutting the heads off parking meters with a pipe cutter in the opening scene. It was the ultimate act of idiotic defiance. But, by opposing nothing, I supposed, he opposed everything. Cinema is a form of immortality, sure, but it's also a type of death: images flickering on the screen forever as we all edge closer to the grave. Later, I got drunk at the Gold Room and went looking for some parking meters to dismember, but I couldn't find any in Echo Park. Instead, I cut up my credit cards and cried.

Game

The name of the game? Let's call it Termite Control. It's a game you—and by "you" I mean "I"—play at home and out of necessity. It requires intense concentration and fortitude: you stare for hours at the hardwood floor in your apartment's living room, letting your eyes relax so you can see the floor—the whole floor—and you wait for any sudden movement, and once you've seen some, you find the hole in the hardwood where the termites are entering, and you cover it with a piece of clear packaging tape. Sometimes this prevents the termites from entering the room for months. Other times, like now, they're back within minutes through another access point. You've played this game nine times tonight, and the night is still young. The only rule: learn to lose. Learn to love to lose. There's no winning this game (a good life lesson). When you move out come summer, someone—your slumlord, or the slumlord's assistant, or even the slumlord's cleaning crew—is going to wander in here and wonder why two-thirds of the apartment's surface area is covered in clear packaging tape. "What the fuck is with the tape?" they might wonder. "And why did this dude leave three boxes of *Twilight Zone* DVDs?" And you'll have no answer to these questions, because by then you'll be long, long gone.

Climate Change

California was behind me, more speck than spectacle. I'd sold everything except for my Triumph and a change of clothes. It was winter, but it felt like spring. The seasons had turned strange. Outside Houston, I was drinking with some old astronauts at the old astronaut bar. One guy had been to space. I asked him what he thought about climate change. He said, "I've been to space." I said, "Yeah, what was that like?" He said, "It's a lot like climate change. No one cares."

Home

I'm standing in the stands of Dodger Stadium in the rain in a dream. It's been raining so long they called the game on account of it, and now all the players and the fans have gone to wherever they go when they're not playing or fanning. I am alone. It's unusually foggy now. I lunge onto the field and into the fog and round the bases. First. Second. When I turn second, the fog begins to lift. Lifts some more. Altogether. When I turn third, that's when I see her, the Virgin Mary, glowing beneath the major-league stadium lights. She reclines at the mouth of the visitor's dugout, near the on-deck circle. She is naked, and her hair is dyed blonde but not down there. She is naked, and she is spreading her legs. She is spreading her legs, and she is calling me home. So, I go. I go home, and the fog returns. The fog returns and the fog returns. Home.

Unending

The market crashed, and so did I. On the Triumph on I-69. Leaving California and headed to Kentucky, hoping to get lucky. I was half-drunk and in Texas. It was totally raining. The wind picked up, and I dropped the bike and skidded into a guardrail. I lived—only minor injuries. But I lost my license and what was left of my pride. Now I'm in recovery. Sobering. And here's the sobering thing about sobering: it never ends. Or, it doesn't end until it ends. Or until I do.

Hey, It's America

33.

I decide to have a festival. I invite Dave and Lisa and the guy I know with guns.

Dave likes to dance. It helps him beat back the blues. Last year, he lost his job as a personal shopper for a coterie of reality show housewives after one of his high-profile clients leaked her own grocery list to TMZ and then blamed Dave when the stunt resulted in a network advertising boycott. Now he works at the Lullaby House on La Brea and hates it. It's the family business. His parents opened the orphanage a year before he was born. A decade later, it crushed nine-year-old Dave to learn that he wasn't an orphan like the rest of the kids. He's felt like an outsider among outsiders ever since.

"I wouldn't say I hate my job," Dave says on the phone tonight. "I enjoy helping orphans. But my parents are unbearable."

"At least they're alive," I say, feeling a sinking sadness and a sense of regret as I say it.

"Go ahead," Dave says. "If you want to talk, I'll listen."

He means do I want to talk about my dead parents again? I don't. "Not tonight," I say.

"Right on," Dave says. "Let's probe to the positive. You're throwing a festival, man!"

My parents were rabid thrill ride enthusiasts, killed in the worst roller coaster accident of the 1980s. I was there that day, but, fortunately for me, I wasn't tall enough to ride. Instead, I stood there, leaning against the guardrail next to my grandparents, gripping a bag of cherry-berry cotton candy as the worst-case scenario unfolded in front of us. I'll skip the horrific details. If you're into morbid stuff, google: "the worst roller coaster accident of the 1980s." It's the first result. But be warned: it is nightmare stuff. Even thirty years later, my savings account flush with the settlement money, I still can't stomach cotton candy. Just the thought of a roller coaster fills me with fear, and when I'm filled with fear, I need a release, and when I need a release, I either get drunk or masturbate (sometimes both). Occasionally: simultaneously. Today, I overdid it, but at least now the fear has subsided for a bit before the guilt will kick in and start the whole tedious pattern over again.

Lisa calls and says my guilt stems from the fact I was brainwashed as a child.

I tell her I was raised by my grandparents. "They were Quakers," I say. "They didn't even push an ideology on me. I don't recall any brainwashing."

"Of course, you don't," she says. "That's one of the hallmarks of brainwashing: not remembering."

I feel uncomfortable considering the prospect of suppressed traumas because many of the memories I do remember are already ugly enough, so I change the subject. "What do you think of my festival?"

"It's fantastic," she says, "but you'll need a name attached to it if you want to generate any buzz."

"A name?" I say.

"Don't worry," she says. "I know a guy who knows Clint Eastwood."

"Didn't Clint Eastwood just call our generation a bunch of pussies?" I say.

"No," she says. "He said that about millennials."

"Aren't we millennials?" I say.

"No," she says, "we do drugs. We're part of a forgotten micro-generation between X and Y."

"What are we called?" I say.

"I forget," she says. "The name isn't memorable, but you know what name is? Clint Eastwood."

"His star is fading," I say.

"Hey," Lisa says, "it's America. A star is a star."

Later, my Spotify goes rogue and plays an early-aughts hit that isn't on any of my playlists. As soon as I hear the initial drum track, I'm transported back to my second semester at Cal State Fullerton when I lived with Dave in a studio above a bakery, and now, listening to the opening synths, I suddenly feel like skipping my History of the Future class, slamming a sixer of Rolling Rock, and eating a day-old bagel sandwich. The name of the song is called "Clint Eastwood." It's by Gorillaz.

Right now, Lisa texts: "Clint Eastwood, yo!"

And I'm like: What? So, I text back: "What? How do you know I'm listening to that, you freak?"

And she writes: "What?"

And I write: "'Clint Eastwood'!"

And she writes: "He's in for your festival. :)"

And I write: "Seriously?"

And she writes: "As serious as dental hygiene."

And then she adds: "Off to floss, boss."

The guy I know with guns always has super original things to say about the Constitution. He also knows obscure stories about the sex lives of the Founding Fathers. For instance, he says that, despite his weird wig and wooden teeth, George Washington ravished more women than the original British Invasion bands. "I mean more chicks than the Beatles and the Stones, combined," he says.

We're standing on the side of the 7-Eleven on Sunset, sipping Coca-Cola Slurpees. "That's fascinating," I say.

"There's a reason we erected a monument to his boner on the National Mall is all I'm saying," he says. "The dude was virile."

"I didn't think he had any children," I say.

"Not biological, but he had his way with an entire nation. Think about it," he says, pointing to the 7-Eleven marquee. "What if I told you this place is named after him?"

"7-Eleven?" I say. "Yeah, right."

"It's true," he says. "George Washington was a colonial spymaster. Probably the single greatest secret agent of the eighteenth century. Guess what his code name was during the Revolution?"

"American Dad," I say.

"Good guess, but no." Again, he points to the 7-Eleven sign. "Agent 711."

"Interesting theory," I say. "However, I think they named it 7-Eleven because they're open from seven a.m. to eleven p.m."

"Sure, that's the official story," he says. "But do some googling. It'll get spooky."

And when I get home, I do. Turns out the guy I know with guns is right about George Washington's Agent 711 nickname during the war. I remove a dollar bill from my wallet and examine his face for several minutes. I bet he was a mean poker player. Just then, I have an idea for my festival so I open the Notes app on my iPhone and type:

711 Fest

But that doesn't make any sense now that I consider it, so I delete it. Then I type:

911 Fest

But that sounds dangerous and misguided, so I delete it. Then I type:

1111 Fest: Make a wish!

My wish is that I could think of a decent name for my festival because this isn't one so I delete it.

I got the idea for my festival because everywhere I went people always told me they were looking forward to my festival. They said: "We're looking forward to your festival, man!" However, I didn't have a festival. It was a case of mistaken identity. I look just like the guy who founded this famous music festival in the desert where the hippest influencers selfie themselves in their expensive sunglasses and unironic rompers. I've never attended the festival myself, but judging by the extravagant partying appearing in my Instagram feed it feels like I'm missing out on some serious fun, so I thought: Why go all the way out to the desert? Why not bring the party to me? Why not be the person people think I am anyway? Thus, my festival—and I hope that it will be even trendier and more influential than that other guy's festival!

I want to invite more people to my festival, but I don't know more people. Aside from Dave and Lisa and the guy I know with guns, most of my friends are either married or dead. On the phone, Dave is reassuring. He says not to worry.

"Don't worry," he says. "I'll bring the orphans. It'll do them well to get out and dance. Will there be dancing at your festival?"

"Of course," I say. "It's a festival. I'm working on the playlist now."

"What's the name of your festival?" Dave says.

"No idea," I say, and right then another random song starts playing on my Spotify. I listen to the first verse. It's about a guy on a horse, and the horse doesn't have a name. "How about I call my festival A Festival with No Name?"

"Hmm," Dave says. "It could work if you're aiming for irony, but everyone hates irony now. These days it's all about positivity and hotness. You should call your festival Burning Ma'am."

"Did you say Burning Ma'am?"

"Yeah," Dave says, "and at the end of the festival, you can torch a wicker woman instead of a wicker man. The future is female. You'll be lauded and loved."

"I don't think so," I say, but I type it into my Notes app anyway because I don't have any better ideas.

MAKE MY DAY with Clint Eastwood Fest

No Idea Fest

Burning Ma'am?

25.

The city weekly called the guy who founded the famous music festival a "provocateur" and a "madman genius." I wonder if you have to be a madman genius at provocation to throw really great festivals or if throwing really great festivals instills these skills. Either way, I hope that my festival will be a wildly provocative event! I've been practicing my madman moves in the mirror.

24.

The guy I know with guns says he can see the madman in me, sure, but if I genuinely want to be considered a genius, I should wise up and get myself an arsenal like him. He says that it's only a matter of time before the shit hits the fan and do I want to be utterly helpless after such a paradigm-shifting event?

"No, no, you do not," he says. "Guns save lives. They are as important as the Constitution itself. Shit, we wouldn't even have a Constitution if it weren't for guns. We'd all be drinking tea all day like d-bags and venerating the damn queen. Fuck the queen."

"How do you really feel?" I say, sipping my Mountain Dew Slurpee outside the 7-Eleven on Sunset.

"Other than this brain freeze," he says, killing his Slurpee, "I don't feel. I'm always rational, always armed. And you know what the experts say about a well-armed populace, right?"

"It's the best defense against tyranny."

"That's right," he says, "and you don't want any tyranny at your festival. You could even call your festival No Tyranny."

"It's called EchoFest," I say.

"Nice," he says.

Lisa texts, "Paul, I'm so excited for your festival."
I text back, "My name isn't Paul, Lisa."
Lisa texts, "You're such a Paul, pal."

22.

Paul is the name of the guy who started the legendary music festival in the desert and otherwise throws really great festivals. He's also got another phenomenal one on a mountain in Ecuador where there isn't any music, and instead of song, everyone stays silent and juice-fasts for the six days leading to the solstice. Then everyone gorges on magic-mushroom tacos and drinks frog-venom tea from crystal chalices and listens to their own crazed interior monologues until they puke their brains out and reconnect with the wide-eyed wonder of their inner children. From what I've read on Reddit, this festival sounds intense and awesome, but I hope that my festival will be even more impressive. There are only six days left, and I still don't have any supplies for my festival. I do, however, have a pretty decent playlist.

I go to the Whole Foods Market in Venice Beach to buy artisanal sandwich supplies for my festival and whom do I meet in the beer cooler but Paul, the guy who throws great festivals.

Paul says, "Dude, I can't wait for your festival!"

I say, "Dude, you're coming to my festival?"

Paul says he wouldn't miss it for the world, which means a lot because he's so worldly. He only dates European auto-show models. "Can't forget the limes," he says, picking up a couple of limes to accompany his case of Corona. "My girlfriend's girlfriend would get all stabby."

"So," I say, "I've got to ask: What's the secret to throwing great festivals?"

Paul sets down the beer, does a short sequence of standing yoga poses, and then he stops and lifts his left arm and begins rotating the limes in the palm of his hand as if they were a pair of Chinese medicine balls. The limes circle themselves slowly in a clockwise rotation through his fingers and I'm transfixed as he completes five full revolutions before reversing the direction.

"Exploitation is key," he says, eventually. "Bottom line: if people aren't exploited, it isn't a great festival."

"Exploitation," I say. "Got it. Anything else?"

"Yes," he says. "Aim for the youth tourism demographic. It's a bull's-eye every time. If you can afford to build out your PR team, do it. Hire some savvy media folks to make you some super sick memes. You'll need a slick tagline, too. And most importantly: sell things at your festival. Lots of things. Do you know the easiest way to sell things?"

I nod like I used to nod at my professors back at Fullerton when I didn't know the answer to something but nonetheless bobbed my head to avoid them calling on me. It worked every time.

"Hot chicks and hashtags," Paul says, answering his own question. "Remember that."

I tap, tap, tap my index finger to my temple. "I'm taking notes."

I unlock my cell, open the Notes app, and hand Paul my phone. "What do you think of this?"

He squints and says, "Burning Ma'am?"

"Sorry," I say, "scroll down."

ECHO

ECHO

ECHO FEST *

@ECHOPARKLAKE

The festival that echoes all of the greatest festivals!

*featuring Clint Eastwood

"It's not bad design," he says. "But it could use a pop of color, and a better tag."

20.

Exploitation. Youth tourism. PR team. Sick memes. A slick tagline. Sell things. Lots of things. Hot chicks and hashtags. A pop of color. Check.

Other than artisanal sandwiches, I can't figure out what to sell at my festival. Dave suggests I sell orphans. He says, "You could sell them to happier homes."

"Think of something else," I say. "You're imaginative."

He says he can't promise anything. He's mostly moronic when it comes to business stuff. "Otherwise," he says, "I'd be speaking to you from my party yacht instead of this awful orphanage."

"Are you still writing your poetry?" I say.

"The other day I did an erasure of my W-2," he says. "But that's about it. My chapbook keeps getting rejected."

"It'll hit," I say. "Unlike me, you've got the gift with words."

"You wrote most of my essays for me at Fullerton," he says.

"But that's a different kind of writing," I say. "What's a catchy tagline for my festival?"

"Let me think on it," he says. "I'll call you back."

Five minutes later, the phone rings, and when I answer Dave asks if I'm ready.

"Hit me."

"Hotter than global warming!" he says. "That's your tag."

"It's definitely memorable," I say, "but it might be a bit arch."

"How about keeping it simple then? THE PARTY OF THE CENTURY. Put it in all caps. Who'd miss that?"

"I'd be afraid to miss that," I say.

"Me too," Dave says.

I get a second opinion on sales tactics from the guy I know with guns since he fancies himself as a tactician of all sorts. He thinks I should sell cheap bump stocks and more affordable AR-15s at my festival. He says that cheap bump stocks and more affordable ARs are hard to come by these days and that I'd be doing good, honest Americans an actual service if I sold them these items at a discount. I tell the guy I know with guns that I don't know where to get any cheap bump stocks or more affordable ARs, and he admits that he doesn't either. "Check this out," I say, handing him my iPhone.

E C H O 🎉 🎉 🎉

E C H O

E C H OFEST*

@ E C H O P A R K L A K E

🎉 *THE PARTY OF THE CENTURY!* 🎉

*featuring Clint Eastwood

"Sweet," he says. "Looks killer. I've got a better slogan though. Try: The most revolutionary cultural experience since the Revolutionary War."

"That's great," I say. It's a lie. I habitually lie to people with guns.

Lisa says since my festival is just a baby festival I should sell tickets to more established festivals at my festival. She says she knows a guy who knows how to get cheap tickets to most festivals. I say why not because I don't have any better ideas. She says I don't have any better ideas because I was brainwashed as a child. My theory as to why I don't have any better ideas is because I drink too much and masturbate and always feel guilty afterward.

"See," Lisa says, "I told you."

16.

I'm feeling guilty right now.

15.

"Say what you will about living in the end times," the guy I know with guns says, "but this sunset is spectacular."

He's right. Tonight, outside the 7-Eleven, the sky is glorious—a purplish pink like the color of a cruise ship drink. Speaking of, we've spiked our Piña Colada Slurpees with strong rum, and this reminds the guy I know with guns about the time Benjamin Franklin got blackout drunk with a prerevolutionary dominatrix and forgot the safe word. "Have I told you this story already?" he says.

"I don't think so," I say. "I think I'd remember it."

"So," he says, "Franklin's at the hottest brothel in Philly in July. We're talking pre-air-conditioning-America here. Plus, Franklin only screwed with his clothes on, so it was even hotter. Have you ever done that?"

"No," I say.

"Makes for a long night," he says. "And it did. Next morning, Benjamin Franklin walks out of the brothel with a pair of broken bifocals, a black eye, and some real pep in his step. Then he goes to sign the Declaration of Independence, because it's July fourth, 1776, but since he can't see the document he's supposed to sign due to his broken bifocals, he gets nervous, which causes everyone else to get nervous, too, and the Founding Fathers are all standing around second-guessing the whole endeavor, but all of a sudden, this mysterious figure in a black robe appears out of nowhere and says, 'Sign that parchment!' And everybody is like: Wait, what? Who the fuck is this guy? Then the mystery man gives this rousing speech which concludes, 'If I were dying right now, you cowards, I'd muster my last ounce of strength and sign that parchment.' And then everybody rushes in and signs the Declaration of Independence, and the rest is literally history. Happy America, America!"

He hands me his flask, and I add more rum to my Slurpee. "Who was this mystery man?"

"Certain folks say it was the alchemist: the Count of St. Germain. Others claim it was the ghost of Francis Bacon and some even argue that it was death incarnate who appeared that day. But most scholars say that the event never happened."

"What do you think?"

"I think it was Agent 711 in disguise. The Maverick of Mount Vernon."

"To George Washington," I say.

"Cheers," he says.

And then it hits me: I'm drunk.

Dave calls the next morning and interrupts my hangover, says, "What name did you land on for your festival?"

I feel like I'm going to die. "I feel like I'm going to die," I say.

He says, "That's the worst name ever for a festival."

"No," I say, summoning my inner–George Washington. "It's called EchoFest."

"Why?"

"It's in Echo Park."

"I get that, but the name fails to properly frame the focus of your festival," he says. "Also: What is the focus of your festival?"

"Focus?" I say. "I can't. I'm wickedly hungover."

"What are you selling at your festival?"

"Tickets to other festivals."

"You could call it Festival Fest," Dave suggests. "I like the alliteration. Change the tag, too: Your ticket to the hottest tickets."

"I don't know how you come up with this stuff on the spot," I say. "That's so good."

"I commune with the divine," Dave says. "I'm also working on a new poetry chapbook. When is your festival, by the way?"

"Saturday."

"This Saturday?"

"Uh-huh."

"The clock is ticking," he says. "You better start your media blitz now."

And so I do.

I go get blitzed on Bloodys at the Gold Room, and then I poster every telephone pole in walking distance. I cover each street in Silver Lake and Echo Park with Festival Fest flyers. Meanwhile, since Dave has wheels, he hits Los Feliz, Highland Park, downtown, and the next day it's up to Glendale, Burbank, and Pasadena. The day after, he heads down to the only cool pocket of Orange County: Santa Ana. "Mission accomplished," he says over the phone afterward.

"Man, I'm still hungover from that rum I drank with the gun guy the other day," I say, sipping my second beermosa of the morning.

"I'm not going to be evangelical about sobriety," he says. "But maybe you could cut back? You might feel better. I do."

"After the festival," I say. "Meanwhile, I just need to power through my weaknesses."

FESTIVAL FEST*

🎉 AKA THE PARTY OF THE CENTURY! 🎉

Your ticket to the hottest (and cheapest) tickets!

This Saturday @ 10 a.m.
@ ECHO PARK LAKE
(by the paddleboats)

*featuring Clint Eastwood

Lisa calls and asks me to remind her of the location of my festival. I say, "Echo Park Lake."

"That's right," she says. "By the paddleboats?"

"Bingo," I say.

Then she asks if I can hold on, and there's a long pause, and I can hear her microwaving something.

Then I hear her eating.

Then I hear her making coffee.

Then I hear her washing dishes.

Then I hear her vacuuming.

Then I hear her turning on a different machine.

Then I hear her having an orgasm.

Then I hear her lighting a cigarette.

Then I hear her taking a shower.

Then I hear her toweling off.

Then I hear her brushing her teeth.

Then I hear her flossing.

She spits and says, "Sorry about that. I like to take a few mindful minutes every couple of hours. Self-care. What time does your festival start?"

I say, "Ten a.m."

"Perfect," she says. "I'll bring the tickets."

The guy I know with guns calls up and says that he's got a boner because Clint Eastwood will be at my festival. He says he admires Clint Eastwood so much because so many Clint Eastwood movies feature such fine weaponry and promote the frontier notion of a rugged individualist sticking it to the collective. The guy I know with guns says that all his friends with guns all love Clint Eastwood, too. "Consider your festival safe from the elements," he says. "I talked to the guys and they're happy to provide security for your festival pro bono."

"I can't thank you enough," I say. "By the way, I've been wrecked since that rum the other night."

"Yes," he says. "That was sort of an experimental batch. I'm still tweaking the recipe."

"You made it?"

"I make all my alcohol," he says. "When the apocalypse comes, we're going to need plenty of booze on hand to stay brave. I also make my own shoes."

Festival morning and Dave is the first to arrive. He shows up with a busload of orphans and tells me they came prepared to dance. "Point us to the dancefloor."

I point to the dancefloor.

"Grass?" he says.

I tell Dave not to tread on me. "Not now," I say. "I haven't had a sip this morning, but you can tread on me all you like after this beer."

As Dave and company dab their way to the grassy dancefloor, I crack open a cold one, press play on my playlist, and America's "A Horse with No Name" gallops through the PA speakers.

"America," Dave says, smiling. "The band. They're from the UK."

9.

Man, these orphans can dance.

8.

Lisa is the next to arrive at my festival. She sets up a booth next to my artisanal sandwich stand. On the table, she has hundreds of tickets to a dozen other festivals: Bonnaroo, Burning Man, Cannes, CMJ, Coachella, Forecastle, Jazz Fest, KCON, Lollapalooza, South by Southwest, Sundance, and something called Fyre Festival.

"I've never heard of that one," I say, tapping the stack of Fyre tix.

"Brand new festival," she says. "It's supposed to be like Coachella on steroids or something. I know the promoter from back in my Manhattan days. He's actually the one who hooked us up with all of these tickets."

"Festival Fest!" I say. "We are the ticket to all of the tickets, and sandwiches."

"And let us not forget the poker-faced advocate of truth, justice, and the American way," Lisa says. "Mr. Clint Eastwood."

"Where is he?" I say.

"He'll be here," she says.

Clint Eastwood isn't the next to arrive at my festival. Instead, a guy on a Triumph motorcycle rides up onto the sidewalk where he parks and removes his helmet. He's got bright blue eyes like a baby wolf, and he seems somehow familiar. Pretty Eyes kisses Lisa on the cheek and acknowledges me with a nod. "Hey man," he says, "is this your festival?"

I nod back.

"New development," he says, handing Lisa a manila envelope. "Mr. Eastwood can't make it. He's making a new movie, but he asked me to send his regrets, and also to give you this. It's cash. He felt bad."

"Are you in the movie?" Lisa asks him.

"No," he says. "I quit acting."

"That's terrible," Lisa says.

"At a certain point," he says, "you just have to be yourself."

For some reason, he looks directly at me when he says this.

"I'm leaving town," he says to Lisa. "For good."

"What?" she says. "When?"

"Monday or Tuesday," he says. "You should stop by tonight, catch up. I have a cornucopia of delectable edibles."

"Are you still in that duplex on Liberty?" she says.

"Not for long," he says.

He leans in again, gives Lisa a peck on the cheek. I reach out to shake his hand, and he grabs my entire arm and leans in, says, "Clint Eastwood knows that Festival Fest will be a big hit. He said to tell you that you've just gotta ask yourself one question now: Do I feel lucky?"

"Yes, I do," I say. "Can I interest you in a sandwich for the road? Perhaps some complimentary Sundance tickets? You're a movie guy."

Pretty Eyes flips the visor down on his motorcycle helmet and I catch my reflection in the mirrored lens. I look like hell.

"That guy is good-looking," I say to Lisa, after he zooms away on his Triumph. "How do you know him?"

"We used to, you know," she says, making an obscene gesture. "Fuck Clint Eastwood for ghosting on us. Seriously."

Just then, twelve bearded dudes in fedoras arrive at my festival. They're wearing matching T-shirts with Clint Eastwood's scowling face on them, and above Clint's head, it says: GOT WOOD?

"Who are you guys supposed to be?" Lisa says to the new arrivals. "The Clint Eastwood fan club?"

"One of many," says the guy in front with the scraggliest of beards. "We're the Newport Beach branch. All the local Woodys are coming today: Hollywood, Burbank, and even Rancho Cucamonga. It's not every day you get to meet the master."

"Welcome to Festival Fest," I say. "We have the cheapest tickets to the hottest festivals as well as an assortment of artisanal sandwiches. The dancefloor is yonder."

But the Clint Eastwood fans just stand there squinting into the sun sans sunglasses, looking fierce.

5.

The guy I know with guns is the next to arrive at my festival. He says, "Actually, I've been here all morning. Maybe you didn't detect me on account of my disguise?"

I look closer and notice that he's wearing a white powdered wig, blue aviators, and a red 7-Eleven T-shirt. For some reason, he's also got a fake mustache plastered over his real mustache. He points to a group of palm trees across the lake. "I've got a guy with guns behind each of those trees," he says, "so everyone is super safe and secure and they will remain so for the duration of your fine festival."

"Thank you for your service," I say, saluting.

He hands me his gun. "Hold my Glock for a sec. I'm gonna cut a rug like a licensed carpet installer."

I play the song "Clint Eastwood" by Gorillaz, and all the Clint Eastwood fans stop standing around scowling and hit the dancefloor.

Turns out, the guy I know with guns can dance. He's got an impressive Running Man / Roger Rabbit combo. Even Dave is impressed. "Woah," Dave says, sidling up. "Who is he?"

"Agent 711," I say. "Festival Fest's Chief Security Officer."

"How do you know him again?" Dave says.

"He's the guy that hangs out at 7-Eleven I told you about."

"Oh, the gun nut."

"That's him."

"Dude can dance."

Soon enough, all sorts of folks are at my festival. Another convoy of Clint Eastwood enthusiasts arrives in a motorcade of old SUVs. A kickball team's worth of Silver Lake hipsters kick off their shoes and dance with Dave and the orphans and the guy I know with guns in the tall grass. A congregation of bearded dudes wander over to Lisa's booth and buy up a bunch of tickets to other festivals. All of a sudden, I'm low on sandwiches. A spontaneous drum circle surrounds the ticket table. The beat is increasingly syncopated and strange. Out of nowhere, a man in a black robe appears and shakes my hand. He introduces himself as Death.

"Is that your first or last name?" I say.

"Just Death," he says. "Is this your festival?"

I nod.

"Festivals are dead," he says, "but even so, this one has a pulse. I can feel it."

"Thank you," I say, reaching out to shake his hand.

"Don't," Death says. Then he turns and strolls through the middle of the drum circle and kills the vibe.

The guy I know with guns grooves over from the dancefloor. "Is he giving you trouble?"

I hand him back his gun. "I don't know," I say. "He says his name is Death."

The guy I know with guns caresses his pistol. "I'll keep an eye on him."

Just then, my Spotify plays a random song that isn't on the

Festival Fest mix: "(Don't Fear) The Reaper" by Blue Öyster Cult jangles through the PA speakers and five minutes later, after the epic song concludes, it starts over again.

That's also when the chanting begins.

3.

Once the chanting starts, there's no stopping it. At first, I think every-one is saying: "We want it. We want it." And I'm thinking: What is it? But then I realize "it" is "Clint."

"We want Clint! We want Clint!"

Lisa shouts into the mic over Blue Öyster Cult, "Mr. Eastwood, unfortunately, can't make it today. He's making a movie, but he sends his deepest regrets, and says to give you this as a token of gratitude for your loyal fanship."

She reaches into the manila envelope and makes it rain singles all over the sidewalk. Instantly, Clint Eastwood fans are fighting other Clint Eastwood fans for Clint Eastwood's cash. They're yanking each other by their beards and pummeling one another in the face. One fan tackles another fan, and they both tumble into the lake and splash each other ferociously in the water.

"Stand back," the guy I know with guns says. "I'll put a stop to this with a warning shot."

He holds the pistol above his head but, just as he pulls the trigger, a Clint Eastwood fan gets punched in the face by another Clint Eastwood fan and falls backward into the guy I know with guns, causing him to misfire, and instead of taking a clear shot at the sky, the bullet shatters a nearby lamppost before ricocheting into the grass dancefloor. Someone screams, "I'm hit." It's Dave. He stops dancing, lifts his left foot, and you can see blood leaking from the back of his ankle, his white Vans turning red.

"Someone call an ambulance," Lisa says.

Death returns to the ticket table, removes an iPhone from his robe pocket, and says, "Hey Siri, call me an ambulance."

Siri says, "Hello, an ambulance."

"Seriously," says Death. "Siri: call 911. This isn't a joke."

Siri abides.

"I'm going to go check on something really quick," the guy I know with guns says. "I'll be right back."

At the edge of the lake, he commandeers a swan-shaped paddle-boat. Then he paddles swiftly to the center of the lake, stops, and drops his pistol overboard. It floats for a minute, before sinking. Afterward, he paddles the rest of the way to the shore, and once arrived, sprints down Glendale Boulevard, leaving only his powdered wig in his wake.

"(Don't Fear) The Reaper" plays for the fourth time in a row and I can't make it stop. Death shreds an air guitar standing on top of the ticket table as various sirens cut through the music, and now my festival is crawling with cops and paramedics. The EMTs tend to Dave as a couple of officers jog over to me with their weapons drawn. The one who looks like he's in charge says, "You want to tell us what's going on here?"

I tell him it's my festival. "Festival Fest," I say.

"Do you have a permit for this festival?" he says.

I tell him I do not, and since I always lie to guys with guns, I tell him that this is the first I've heard anything about a festival permit.

"Sorry," his partner says, "we're going to have to haul you in and shut down this illegal festival."

He's handcuffing me when we hear someone hiding behind a palm tree scream, "Death to tyranny!" followed by a rifle report. The cop who looks like he's in charge clutches his chest and says, "I'm bleeding, bad." Then he drops to the ground.

Now there's a swarm of cops surrounding the ticket table. I step back into the grass and out of the way.

The cops fire into the palm trees and the palm trees fire back.

Then all the orphans are crying, and the Clint Eastwood fans are crying, too. Lisa does her best to console the most hysterical criers. The paramedics load Dave into an ambulance on a gurney, and as they do, Dave says, "I don't have insurance. Am I going to be able to afford this ride?"

The EMT closes the back of the ambulance and speeds away, narrowly avoiding hitting a sad orphan.

Meanwhile, the shootout continues.

The cops fire into the trees and the trees fire back.

The cops fire into the trees and the trees fire back.

Man, these handcuffs hurt.

1.

I'm feeling bad for Dave and worse for the cop who's bleeding out beneath the ticket table, when Paul, the guy who throws really great festivals, shows up flanked by a couple of winsome brunettes in short black dresses, red heels, and redder lipstick. Paul points to his right and says, "This is my girlfriend, Maya." He points to his left. "This is Maya's girlfriend, Adriana."

"Nice to meet you," I say. "I'd shake your hands if I weren't handcuffed."

Paul's all smiles. "This festival is an absolute disaster. You did it, bud!"

"Did what?" I say.

"You failed bigtime," Paul says. "And in America, failures of this magnitude are rarely forgotten, especially when it comes to festivals. Festival Fest will go down as one of the worst festivals in the history of festivals. I'm calling it now: you'll be famous. Well, infamous."

I attempt to loosen the handcuffs, but somehow manage to tighten them. "Ouch," I say.

Maya whispers something in Paul's ear and Paul whispers something in Adriana's ear, and Adriana nods gravely. "All right," Paul says, "we're going to take a little romantic paddleboat ride since we'd prefer not to get shot."

"Thanks for coming to my festival," I say.

∞.

After Paul and the automotive showroom models paddle away, I just take it all in, feeling validated for once in my life. It's the first time I've smiled in years. Death appears and hugs me. "Your parents are so proud of you," he says.

"My parents are dead," I say.

"You say that like it's a bad thing," Death says. "Let's get you out of those handcuffs."

He reaches into his robe pocket and produces a key shaped like a skeleton. Somehow the key fits and the cuffs come right off. I'm feeling good, great even. I am the champion of failed festivals—the maddest of madman geniuses. I finally matter, I think, as a stray bullet clips me in the neck. Amazingly, I don't feel the bullet, but I hear it. The shot rings and rings. It's music to my ears.

American Literature

American Literature

Most days, like most folks, I work. At night, I sit around and have a drink and read some American literature.

I'll admit: Whenever I type "Western Canon" I accidentally add an extra *n*. This, I understand, is my subconscious mind critiquing American literature.

Western Cannon.

Go ahead. It's okay. I'm wearing a motorcycle helmet and a Melville T-shirt.

Go ahead and fire me from the Western Cannon! I'll soar over Iowa City, across the Grand Canyon, and into the lost libraries of the sea.

Sometimes, when I'm driving, I'll hear American literature on the radio and think: Man, if this is what passes for American literature these days we are fucked! But then I realize I'm not listening to American literature. I'm listening to the news.

You won't find American literature in the news unless you're Ezra Pound.

Pound who said: Literature is news that stays news.

Make it new(s).

One time I found American literature at a casino in Elko, Nevada: a Norton anthology hiding in a motel drawer where the Bible should've been.

Although the Bible technically isn't American literature, it's always the best-selling book in America, year in and year out.

Every year I tell myself: "This is the year. This is the year I'll make a significant contribution to American literature." But in reality, I make a minor contribution to my local NPR station and move on.

Speaking of moving on, they say that there are only two plots in American literature: (1) character comes to town, and (2) character leaves town. The third plot, of course, is an amalgam of the two: character comes to town, and leaves. The term "plot" also means a small parcel of land in a cemetery.

Where would American literature be if it weren't for the road?

The automobile is a literary device. It's the motor of so many books—the engine. Matter of time before the wheels come off, though.

Like it or not there is a direct correlation between the price of books and the cost of gas.

All the films adapted from American literature into American movies. Will someone please adapt this book already?

The other day I walked out of a movie theater and into the light.

The other day I was out fighting illiteracy at a neighborhood pub, but it turned out badly because it turns out this particular illiterate was strong and armed.

An Anthology of Twentieth-Century American Illiterature.

Kurt Cobain took pride as the king of illiterature.

Cobain who loved reading William S. Burroughs.

Burroughs who enjoyed cutting apart American literature.

They called him a dope fiend with a pair of scissors.

All modern American literature comes from one book by Mark Twain called *Huckleberry Finn*. Said Ernest Hemingway.

Most of Hemingway's inspiration came from one drink called the mojito.

Tonight, I think I'll whip up a batch of mojitos and read some Hemingway.

Good rum is the foundation of a good mojito.

The Declaration of Independence is the foundation of American literature.

Although some say Franklin invented American literature before Jefferson.

Benjamin Franklin, who never drank a mojito, but loved strong ale. America's first great human of letters, according to David Hume.

What does it mean to be a human of letters in an era where no one writes letters anymore?

Someday they will say of our writers: He was a man of emails. She was a woman of tweets. They were a poet of Instagram. And so on.

Someday we will view the novel as a novelty item.

Poems by and for robots.

Mem(e)oirs.

An age which is incapable of poetry is incapable of any kind of literature except the cleverness of a decadence. Warned Raymond Chandler.

Because even the bluest poet in the reddest state is still prone to the purplest of prose.

Because the internet of the future exists today.

Because it's hard to find American literature in the comment sections on the internet, but sometimes you'll see it in the articles above.

As above, so below.

The cyber-hermeticism of American literature in action.

I can't help but read every comment on the internet as a commentary on the internet itself.

I can't help but read American literature as a commentary on literature itself.

The role of the critic in American literature is to coin consumer expectations.

The role of the consumer is to open their wallets and close their eyes.

Last night, I fell asleep reading.

This morning, I woke up and wrote this line here.

Man, if this is what passes for American literature these days we are fucked!

If a nation's literature declines, the nation atrophies and decays. Warned Pound.

As the language decays, every sentence becomes a death sentence.

American literature never stopped an execution, but it may have prevented a few murders, and it's certainly gotten many of us laid.

Is it possible to find salvation in literature? Maybe. Sure. Why not?

Our literature is a substitute for religion, and so is our religion. Remarked Eliot.

Remarks are not literature. Said Stein.

Here's a bit of gossip: All literature is gossip. Claimed Capote.

It takes a great deal of history to produce a little literature. Observed James.

Even so, it doesn't mean that American history is literature.

Even so, it doesn't mean that American literature is history.

A Novel Idea

The boy wanted to write flash fiction. It was his calling. He told his dad as much one December afternoon in the den upon returning home from boarding school for the break. "Flash fiction?" his dad said, lowering the newest *New Yorker* from his face as his rose-tinted monocle dropped in disgust. The fireplace hissed. "What those degenerates on the internet write? No, no, that won't do. No son of mine is going to produce small works destined for obscurity. Novels: that's the idea. It's a novel idea. Novels longer than your hair, son. Something to make the publishers swoon. Now get to your room and don't come out until you've written a blockbuster."

The boy went into his room, and he didn't come out.

For many years, he didn't come out.

Once emerged, the boy was no longer a boy and still not quite a man. He had hair to his knees but none on his chest. He was twenty-seven. The world had changed. The boarding school had been boarded up. Dad was dead and gone. And the novel? It was not bad. It was not good. But it was not bad. It was like a lot of novels. They loved it in New York.

Past Perfect

I had been drinking and was driving. My wife hadn't shaved because she never showed her legs. We had fought all afternoon. I hadn't been crying because I hide my feelings. The sun hadn't risen because it was night. I had been sleeping with another woman and felt good because she had come. At the same time, I felt bad because I had cheated. She had already left. I had already showered. I had already sobered. I had been feeling hopeful because I had written.

Dogs Named Desire

We got lucky and left Kentucky. This was after our Monday-night marriage, when we lit out for the left coast and struck it rich along the way peddling new sins to Protestants, got blackout drunk at a bar around the corner from the Alamo, forgot everything (including the Alamo) for weeks, and then continued west until we reached the San Fernando Valley where we settled amongst the modest pornographers and the unending strip-mall sprawl. Our love grew small, but our backyard swimming pool loomed largely. We named it Denial and, although we never swam in the damn thing, we liked to lounge next to it and boat drink ourselves into oblivion. Sure, when we sobered there was still plenty wrong with us, but the truth is brighter than the sun sometimes. It's only natural to look away. We did until we didn't. Then we didn't.

She took most of the money and then hooked up with an itinerant yoga instructor and, last I imagined, they were wandering the world inventing new sexual maneuvers.

Meanwhile, I bought some cheap speed and got to work on an uninspired screenplay about a family of disabled acrobats who, despite it all, hang on and hunker down as they learn the true meaning of the holidays, and, sure enough, the saps over at the Hallmark Channel pounced on it and advanced me enough cash to charge a new Charger and put some road under it. I should've gone to Montana. I should've gone to Idaho, but no, I got sentimental and beat it down to the Gulf of Mexico. When I reached the shores of Alabama, there were firemen everywhere. Smoke on the water and the flames into the sky. The heat scorched the sand into glass. I wanted to stick around, to stay and help those folks fight, but instead, I took the unexamined heaviness in my heart and the cash in my jean jacket pocket over to the dog track in Pensacola. I bet it all on a black dog named Desire and dammit if I didn't lose as usual.

Then, I did what they say you shouldn't do: I went home again, and I rented a studio apartment above a bar by Churchill Downs. Beneath me, people bonded over bourbon and beer. Me, I just listened to the lies through the frail floorboards, for weeks. Eventually, I dug myself from that dark place and went downstairs to bask in the neon. At the lip of the bar sat my ex-wife's father. He was kind enough to act dumb about his daughter and me, and so he bought me a beer and then he offered me a job. I was in no position to pass.

The job was janitorial. Nights we cleaned skyscraper offices overlooking the Ohio. The days? They were there, too, always changing. Then it was October, and the Commonwealth light began to fade. A windstorm arrived and knocked out power to the city. For a solid week, I sat there in the dark, trying to think of something besides myself. I thought about driving down to the Sherman Minton Bridge and taking a leap, but for some reason, when the power returned, something inside me lit up, too. Yes, it seemed there were still stories to raise and hell to write. For a while, I palled around with the father until his hands swelled from all the heart pills. By the holidays, he'd stopped coming to work altogether. He had an angioplasty and then died. It hurt when my ex-wife didn't attend the funeral, but it hurt less when the old man left me some money.

More days, not worth naming. In the newspaper, a debate over the merits of bridge building lasted many years. One day I woke up and everyone looked younger. One day I woke up and I was taking a hammer to my birth certificate. One day I woke up and decided to find some hero for a friend. I decided to get a dog. I thought it would love me unconditionally, fill the cheap vacancy in my life.

I went to the shelter and picked out an albino greyhound: one blue eye, one red. She was strange and beautiful. I named her Desire, loaded her into the backseat of the Charger, and drove over to Frisbee Field. That night, the sun was setting rather cinematically behind a stand of elms at the top of the hill. Immediately, she took off after a bird, knocked me over, and took the leash with her. Man, she could fly. I said: Stop, don't.

But she went.

And never came back.

Instant Classic

So suddenly I felt so old.

Midnight at the
Bethlehem Bar & Grille

1984 BC

From the smoking section came a trio of wise men dressed as wise guys in Adidas tracksuits. They carried gifts of Goldschläger, Tic Tacs, and Skoal, and they stood there stupidly, staring at my wife writhing on the floor by the foosball table. When the doctor arrived, he extracted a stethoscope from his satchel, followed by a pair of pilot's headphones, and said: "Damn this birth is loud!" It was true. The jukebox blasted Def Leppard as buzzed bridesmaids squealed into their tequila shots and a couple of coked-out car guys argued about the innocence of John DeLorean, but now all you could hear was a brand-new voice screaming into the world like it already hated the place. If you shut your eyes, everything sounded so severe, but if you opened them just right and let them readjust to the beer light, you could see the makings of a miracle as it happened. And it happened to be a boy, or at least we thought so for many years—until he began running around with prostitutes and tax collectors and raising the dead like a roof.

The Big H

"Stop me if you've heard this one before," Playboy says. "A priest, a rabbi, a Buddhist monk, and Donald Trump walk into a bar."

"Trump?" says Bill. "He doesn't drink. Besides, I know the punch line. He's president." He's sitting shirtless in front of the motel mirror in chinos and a shoulder holster, his dyed hair damp from the shower.

"Hair looks good black," Bill says to the mirror, but Playboy can't tell if he's talking about black hair in general or if he's referring to his own.

Playboy asks Bill if he perhaps left out a pronoun in the previous sentence and Bill extends three fingers, says, "Read between the lines."

"All right," Playboy says. "You look like a top."

Bill says nothing.

Bill says, "Scissors?"

Bill says, "Did you find the scissors?"

"Playboy," Bill says, "any luck with the scissors, any?"

"No," Playboy says. "I'll use your pocketknife."

"It isn't a pocketknife," Bill says. "It's a Swiss Army."

"Cool story, bro," Playboy says. He opens the blade and presses his thumb down stupidly.

"Sharp," he says.

Bill shrugs, says, "That's the point."

"Mind if I smoke?"

"I prefer a barber who smokes."

Playboy lights a Lucky, asks Bill how he wants it.

"No homo," Bill says.

Playboy reminds Bill that he, Playboy, bats for the other team and that it's the twenty-first century and that maybe Bill should learn to be more innovative concerning his hatreds.

Bill says nothing.

Bill says, "Take a little off the sides and front, and a lot off of the back."

Bill says, "Whatever you do, don't do a mullet."

Bill says, "No mullets, okay? I'm looking to meet a nice piece at the casino tonight so don't get hilarious here. Keep it cool."

"I'm Coltrane," Playboys says, as the cutting commences, but it's more like sawing. Eventually, a long black lock of Bill's hair comes loose and falls to the floor.

"Jesus," Bill says.

"You all right?" Playboy asks.

"I'm fine, but take it easy," Bill says. "I need a haircut, not a scalping."

Playboy apologizes. "Sit back, relax, and let the Old Navy do what it does best."

"Swiss Army," Bill says. "Old Navy's something else. A store."

Playboy tongues his cigarette over to the corner of his mouth and lets it hang there so he can cut and smoke at the same time. Smoking without appendages, it's an old trick Playboy picked up in the club, back when he was a bass player in a Judas Priest tribute band.

"Jesus," Bill says. "Jesus H. Christ."

"You all right there, William?"

"I'm fine," Bill says. "I was just thinking about Jesus."

"After Malibu, you're considering a career change?"

"Not at all," Bill says. "I was thinking about that name: Jesus H. Christ. What does the *H* stand for?"

"Harold?" Playboy wagers. "Disciples called him Harry maybe? Like the prince?"

"That," Bill says, "does not ring."

"Then it's probably Hank," Playboy says. "Hank's the perfect name for gods and dogs."

"Uh-uh," says Bill. "No."

Playboy saws off another lock. He's working the back, by Bill's neck, and leaving him with a little rattail. "Do you have any theories as to the *H*?"

"Holy is my best guess," Bill says. "And Holy shit that hurt."

"My bad," Playboy says.

"Jesus-Holy-Christ," Bill says. "It sounds stupid enough to be true. The big mystery is solved."

Playboy stops cutting, steps aside and admires the dark mound of hair on the ground. "How's it look?"

"Doing fine," Bill says. "Maybe more off the back, though. The back is sort of, you know, I don't know."

"You don't dig the rattail?"

"No," Bill says. "I do not."

"Personally," Playboy says, "I think the ladies will love it. It's ironic nouveau. Hipster chicks in droves."

"Now you're speaking my language," Bill says. "You ever had any honeypot?"

Playboy doesn't dignify that with a response. Instead, he continues cutting, now and then pausing to ash his square onto the pile of hair.

"Are you a believer?" Bill says, out of the blue.

Playboy considers it, says, "Do you mean: Do I believe in Jesus H. Christ?"

"Bingo," Bill says. "Jesus or God or Buddha or Zeus or whatever the hell—do you believe any of that?"

"I don't know," Playboy says, stamping out his cigarette. "I don't think about it much. I guess if there's a God, I'd call that a surprise ending. How about you?"

"The only thing I believe in is avoiding chicks with spider tattoos," Bill says and laughs.

Playboy laughs, too, even though he's not sure if or why it's funny. "I thought that spiders are good luck," Playboy says, and as he says it a little spider crawls across the motel mirror. "Look. See that? That's called synchronicity right there."

Bill reaches out and smashes the spider with his thumb.

"You shouldn't have done that," Playboy says. "It's bad mojo."

"Only if you're a superstitious cocksucker," Bill says.

A sudden panic surges through Playboy's arm, and he drops the knife. This feeling is more than an opinion. It's either a heart attack or fear. He steps back from Bill and takes an inventory of the room. It's an orgy of peach wine coolers, High Life cans, and Thai takeout boxes. Nothing strange. Nothing to see or worry about. Playboy strikes another Lucky Strike, and soon enough he's at the window, peering through the plastic blinds. The parking lot is empty, and the empty spaces look to him like a framework for something he can't quite pinpoint. Agnosticism maybe? He gets the feeling that something is missing. He says to Bill: "Hey buddy, where's the backpack? You know the one that we're not supposed to let out of our sights, like, ever?"

Bill stares at himself in the mirror and runs his gnarled fingers through his new hairdo. Eventually, he says: "The trunk? The backpack is in the trunk. Shit, man, I don't know."

The last time Bill didn't know shit was a week ago, outside Barstow, when Playboy asked him if the sheriff's deputy was dead.

"I don't know," he said. "Probably. I shot him."

Now Playboy is feeling a twinge of déjà vu.

There's a knock at the door, followed by another.

Bill flashes his Beretta and says, "You expecting anyone?"

Then Playboy picks up the pocketknife and says, "No one I know."

Three Prayers for Artists

Almighty Branch Manager, please gaze favorably from your franchise in the sky and bestow a satisfactory employee rating upon this starving sandwich artist who has not only affirmed his commitment to unironically following the company account on Twitter but also vowed to serve the freshest five-dollar footlongs imaginable. Give him Adderall, Ativan, Klonopin, Vicodin, and whatever other street drugs it takes for him to make a decent sandwich on an annual salary that's much lower than an actual artist's yearly salary; and strengthen all of us sub-club customers in our resolve to trust in the wisdom of high-quality produce, excellent customer service, and low operating costs. May we all eat fresh in the service of slim waistlines and the Lord; in a new corporate jingle's name, we pray. Five. Five dollar. Amen.

FOR CON ARTISTS

Oh God, the great private eye in the sky, we respectfully ask that you stop tailing us and, moreover, we pray for your forgiveness. Oh Lord, we admit that the good spirit has not always guided us and that we've spent decades picking pockets, cheating tax collectors, and fleecing newbs with everything from fool's gold necklaces to timeshares on the moon. True, but all that badness is behind us. Now we're asking you for your almighty assistance: it is our great pleasure, Lord, to pray to you and present a modest business proposal for your consideration. It is our great pleasure, Lord, to pray to you and ask you to assist us in the transfer of eleven million five hundred thousand US dollars to your bank account in heaven. Heavenly Father, should you decide to render your services in this regard you would be paid thirty-three percent of the total funds for your assistance. Reply with a rotisserie of gift cards if you are willing to work with us. Amen.

Oh God, we are running out of ideas! We just realized the concept of the universe is the only concept! Now we are echeloning our notions and acknowledging you as the fundamental one, oh Lord, but we'd like to note that the first word in "concept" is "con," which seems suitable given the long con you've pulled on the universe with your eternal silence. Oh, we are listening to you listening to us listening to you. Oh, this is a portrait of you because we say so. It is a diamond-encrusted skull: a memento mori for an immortal. It is a sculpture of a urinal in a museum somewhere in heaven. It is a chair where no one sits, next to the definition of the word "chair." It is also a prayer without a prayer. Amen.

Deadhorse

Outside, the snow falls like commercial fishers falling from boats. It's almost April here in Alaska, and although the local marijuana industry is booming, our head shop is about to bust. Today, you say, is an excellent name for a dog, and you're allergic to dogs. Earlier I mistook a beer for the mirror, and now I'm wondering about California: What is the state of California? When we left, there was almost nothing left. Now we're half past hungry in the Land of the Midnight Sun, but instead of setting the table, you set the teenage psychic's business card on the table, and I set both the business card and the table on fire. Because, when you live in a place called Deadhorse, every possibility is already exhausted. And so am I.

The Summer He Went Swimming

after Loudon Wainwright

THE BACKSTROKE

That summer he did the backstroke, naked in his neighbor's pool, while his neighbors were off dreaming in some faraway version of Kennebunkport. He swam the backstroke, naked in his neighbor's pool, one night while contemplating his recent attempts at facial hair. The beard had failed miserably—the mustache: worse. He swam the backstroke, naked in his neighbor's pool, one night, while his neighbors were away in some distant Kennebunkport, dreaming, as he contemplated his doomed facial hair endeavors.

It was a very clear night here, very far from Kennebunkport.

His pubic hairs glistened in the banana moonlight and his water-logged dick shriveled beneath the movie-review stars.

And he resolved to try harder.

Keep at it.

Perhaps a goatee.

Maybe a soul patch.

No, not a soul patch.

<<< * >>>

THE BREASTSTROKE

That summer he did the breaststroke, naked, and there wasn't any water involved. Well, that isn't exactly true. The human body consists of sixty percent water.

Correction: That summer he did the breaststroke, naked, and there was sixty percent water involved.

(Her breasts in the midnight moonlight were like teakettles, twin teakettles—where he laid his head and dreamed of some far-away version of Kennebunkport. That place where we all end up someday, when we die.)

<<< * >>>

THE BUTTERFLY

That summer he swam the butterfly in a small, overly urinated public pool, as the small, overly urinated public pool broke from a chrysalis and became a perfectly chlorinated, Olympic-sized pool in Kennebunkport.

Perhaps this was a dream he had?

Yes, it was.

Correction: that summer he dreamed he swam the butterfly in a small, overly urinated public pool, as the small, overly urinated public pool broke from a chrysalis and became a perfectly chlorinated, Olympic-sized pool in Kennebunkport.

<<< * >>>

THE OLD AUSTRALIAN CRAWL

That summer, he did the old Australian Crawl, but it looked so damn American, so new, so ambiguous, so much like Kennebunkport.

<<< * >>>

THE SWAN DIVE

That summer he did a fifty-foot swan dive into a reservoir, and as he dove, he thought how beautiful it was that swans mate for life, but then he wondered what happens if one of the mates dies. Do widowed swans remarry, he asked, or do they move to Kennebunkport?

<<< * >>>

THE CANNONBALL

That summer, at a cocktail party in Kennebunkport, he did a fully clothed cannonball when no one was looking. And it pissed people off.

So he did it again, and again, and again.

Eventually, the people of Kennebunkport grew accustomed to it and learned to embrace it, as the good people of Kennebunkport always do.

<<< * >>>

That summer he sprang from a Rhode Island high-dive in a pair of golden Speedos. Then he bent in midair, touched his toes, and straightened out immediately before entering the water.

It was perfect.

When he emerged, it was December in Kennebunkport, and his golden Speedos had turned silver.

Afterward, he resolved to not jackknife again and vowed never to return to Kennebunkport.

Soon enough, it was Christmas in Texas, and he was mostly sober.

State Secrets

WHEN IN ROME

Proceed to the nearest orifice and enter.

<<< * >>>

ROME WASN'T BUILT IN A DAYDREAM

I tried to build Rome in a daydream. Failed. Tried again. Failed again. Rome wasn't built in a daydream. However, Paris, Tennessee, was.

<<< * >>>

SOUTH OF ROME

All roads lead to Rome, so I took one, but it happened to be a toll road and I didn't happen to have any cash on me, so I ended up south of Rome, but I met some very nice people there.

<<< * >>>

IV

To a nurse an IV is one thing, but to a Roman it is four things!

<<< * >>>

WHEN IN SOUTH ROME

Do as the Southern Romans do: build crucifixes and coliseums and worship Jupiter on Saturdays.

<<< * >>>

ANCIENT KNOCK-KNOCK JOKE

Knock-Knock!
Who's there?
Jupiter!
Jupiter who?
Jupiter hurry, or you'll miss the crucifixion and the orgy!

<<< * >>>

TWO ABHORRENT ROMANS

Baskerville and Polanski.

<<< * >>>

ANCIENT DIARY ENTRY: 4 JUNE 474

And to think they said I was wasting my fucking life when I said I
was going into vandalism!

On Acid

I glance at our guru's finger as he's pointing at the moon, but then I realize it's his middle finger pointed at a riot cop and it's the middle of the afternoon.

On Broadway

I brunched with an acrobat. A nearby boy became a robot. Atop a building, two men pretended they were birds—fell, died, and were buried. The smell of jet fuel permeated. We had ideas about chemtrails and dreamed up ironic epitaphs. We heard sirens screaming, saw pigeons exploding into Alka-Seltzer.

And we knew that, at any moment, songs would burst into people again.

All Americans

Hastings had his repeater leveled at my lungs. I said, "Elevate your aim, son." He was a little older, but I had him smoked by rank. "Something about those hills scares me," he said. "The shadows are strange. I intend to light them up and see what's what, Captain." I said, "Hey, have at it." The sunlight was fading fast. We were outside a city with a name I couldn't pronounce. It was one of the ones with the word "bad" at the end, and this village was worse. It had a name, too. Our translator told us. "Here comes some local talent right now," he said. From a mud hut, a lady emerged in robes and tears. She held her child aloft like a prized bass and chattered away in Pashto. There was a sadness to her words and an urgency in her eyes. I told the translator to figure out what it was she wants. He translated. He said, "She says, 'There is no future here.' Her son has no future. She says she has no future either. She wants you to take the boy to America." "Uh-uh," I said. "Tell her the Tenth Mountain boys are a lot of things, but one of the things we aren't is a goddamn adoption agency." The translator translated, but who knows what he said because, next thing I knew, Hastings was holding the kid and the sad mother was pedaling an ancient ten-speed up the dirt road and into the sunset. I'd never seen someone pedal a bicycle so fast. It was something else. It was snowing in the mountains, and we stood there feeling stupid and cold as nightfall fell all around. "Ideas?" I said. "Anyone?" Hastings rocked the kid to sleep in his arms and said, "I bet I can teach him to shoot. He looks like a stone-cold little dude, a sniper in diapers." Hastings had an understudy now. All winter long at the base, he taught the toddler to volley and aim and zero his scope. The kid was a crack shot, too. In Kandahar that spring, he shot a wild boar between the eyes one afternoon and later that night he shot our translator through the neck by mistake. I was openly surprised and secretly pleased because I never liked that guy. "Each beginning comes from an ending," I said to the boys after the translator died by the dugout of our makeshift softball field. Back then, I was always plagiarizing the great philosopher Seneca in conversation because I'd never had any original thoughts in my head and so, when our tour ended, I stayed on for another. I thought: Hey, maybe we'll catch the rotten cocksucker who took down the towers this time around. It turns out I was wrong. Meanwhile, Hastings took leave. He resumed life and wife stateside and assumed custody of the kid in a Fort Collins, Colorado, courtroom. Then he quickly set to work teaching his adopted son everything he knew besides firearms, which wasn't much, and so he sent the boy to school. On the playground, he learned the crossover dribble and an unblockable rainbow shot from the deep perimeter. Now he's all grown up into an All-American at the University of Kentucky, a true freshman at the two guard. Man, he can shoot. He could always shoot. He takes after his adopted dad. They say he's a lock for a lottery pick after his efforts in the Final Four. As for me, I fell out of the army and into the private sector overseas. For someone like me, it's easy money and a lot of it at that and, despite the exaggerated reports, I am possibly half-nuts but entirely alive.

Kilroy

He went west.

His wife was there. Somewhere.

Days sputtered and stalled. Nights collapsed. The windshield spidered and cracked. The road looked fucked.

Still, he drove. He drove all day. Night. And then some.

After the sunset, there was another sunset. His helmet phone hummed. He toggled the talkbox, speakered the lobe: heard birds—gulls?—and then someone said through a low voice modulator: "Kilroy?"

"Yes. Who's this?"

"Pull over. Now! Then get out of the car. Slow. Don't be a hero. They don't last."

"What?"

"Are you pulled over?"

"No."

"Get out of the car, hero."

"Uh-uh."

"Are you out yet?"

"Hold on."

"Now look around. Do you see me?"

"It's too dark. There were two sunsets tonight. I don't see anything."

"But I see everyone, you see? I see everyone at once, including you. Night vision, baby. I love the future! I didn't even invent it. I'm just living in it. Living in it and loving it."

"Who's this?"

"Your future boss, boss. I'm everyone's future boss. The name's Mister Donny."

"Mister Donny? Is this a job interview, Mister Donny?"

"If I said no, I'd be lying."

"How am I doing?"

"You're hired. Congrats. Don't fly off half-cocked on me now."

"What?"

"What, what?"

"Are you high?"

"Affirmative. I'm on what God's on, son."

"What's the prescription? My teeth hurt. I could use something."

"Infinite power and light. Infinite. That means immeasurable to no end. You cannot measure the power and light that I speak of. If you tried to measure it, you would fail. Don't try it. You're too dim and powerless and inept to attempt it, so unless you want more dimness and powerlessness to fall upon your ass forever, you'll do as you're told. For now, drive. Drive in a westward direction and keep on driving. Drive until you reach the bridge to the Island of California. You'll receive further instructions when you reach the farthest point. Ciao for now."

Kilroy powered down his helmet.

The sky decreased.

The clouds quaked.

What was left of his mind raced.

And the night, it lasted for days.

<<< * >>>

After the wars, they reprogrammed him. They reprogrammed him
after the wars because he needed help. They were there to help repro-
gram him every day because he needed so much help. They helped
so much.

<<< * >>>

He took medicine.

It was for his mouth.

The pills struck a soft chord, mood-wise, and made him drive
slow, real slow. That damned dentist had replaced his front teeth with
rake tines. Since the surgery, he'd developed a strange taste for dirt.
He pulled over. Dug a hole. Ate some dirt. Dug deeper. Ate more
dirt. Some worms. Spit out the worms. More dirt.

A vulture circled above.

Kilroy swallowed, spat, cursed. He speakered his helmet phone.
Dialed out.

"Dr. Spatz's office. Rita speaking."

"Is he in?"

"May I ask who is calling?"

"Anton Kilroy."

"And what is this regarding, Mr. Kilroy?"

"Well, Rita, I was in last week for a standard root canal, and I
believe there's been a mistake. A terrible mistake."

"A mistake?"

"Yes, my front teeth are gone, Rita. They've been replaced with
some sort of metal spikes."

"Spikes?"

"Yes, they appear to be rake tines, Rita. Like the kind you'd find
on a hand rake, for instance. Picture those as your teeth."

"My goodness. I'm afraid the doctor is out of the office this evening, but I'll have him call you first thing in the morning."

"But it's been night here for several days."

"Night? Where are you, Kilroy?"

"Due east of west. Near the Island of California."

"Interesting. Here in Heart Attack Country, it's been evening for several evenings."

"Strange weather, ma'am, but the other reason I called . . . aside from the fangs . . . I've been eating dirt."

"Eating dirt?"

"Uh-huh. Yes."

"Why?"

"I don't know."

"Okay, well, keep eating it. And I'm sure the doctor will have a perfectly reasonable explanation for all of this. He is, after all, a family dentist. Do you have a family, Mr. Kilroy?"

"I do not."

"Have you ever entertained the notion of having a family?"

"I have."

"Well, hold out hope. Speaking of, can you hold?"

"Yes."

He held. He watched a vulture flying a corkscrew pattern in the sky above his car. It was hypnotic.

"Kilroy?"

"Yes."

"I'll have Dr. Spatz call you tomorrow."

"But that could be days!"

"I hope not. I'm tired of watching this damn sunset. And I'd like to get off work someday."

"Thanks."

"No, thank you."

"No, thank you."

"No, thank you!"

"No, thank you, too!"

"No, no thank you, too!"

<<< * >>>

He went back to the wars sometimes. And sometimes, when he went back to the wars, he was at peace with the wars. And sometimes, when he went back to the wars, he was at war with the wars. And sometimes, when he went back to the wars, he was at war with his peace with the wars. Sometimes, when he went back to the wars, he lived through the wars. And sometimes, when he went back to the wars, he died in the wars. And sometimes, when he went back to the wars, he both lived and died in the wars. Because it's possible to both live and die in a war. Quite possible. He was living proof. That was Kilroy. He was here. Kilroy was. Here. But also there.

<<< * >>>

There were flowers then. The wife would water them with a plastic cantaloupe. There were no more bees. There was no more honey. Everyone was allergic to everything.

Kilroy would hug the wife, and she would sneeze. "Bless you," he would say, and he would sneeze.

"Bless you," she would say, and she would sneeze.

"Gesundheit," he would say, and he would sneeze.

"Gesundheit," she would say, and she would sneeze.

This went on for many months until the bees returned.

But, by then, Kilroy had left for the wars.

<<< * >>>

Kilroy was on the side of the road eating dirt when his helmet phone hummed. The night had lightened. The sky was something else. Morning.

"Kilroy here."

"Morning, Kilroy, this is Dr. Spatz returning your call. Now can you explain to me in legalese the nature of your affliction? Rita mentioned something about soccer cleats."

"I'm afraid I don't speak legalese."

"What the hell did they teach you in law school, then?"

"I never went to law school. I went to prison. Then I went to fight in the wars, the Pay-Per-View Wars."

"Ah, a TV vet, I see. Well, soldier it to me instead. Spit it to me from the grave, private."

"There's been a mistake."

"Elaborate."

"My front teeth. They've been replaced. They've been replaced with rake tines. Metal ones of the garden variety."

"Handheld or plow?"

"Handheld, I think. Small."

"Oh, that's no mistake, my boy. That was intentional. Orders. You see I follow those things."

"Orders?"

"Yes, sir. They trickle down from the top."

"How high?"

"Trump Tower. Office of the Plastic Surgeon General. He made us dentists swear a new oath. The poor health of our patients shall be our first commitment. We shall use our professional knowledge according to the laws of nature. That's Darwin, son. And I'm afraid survival isn't in the cards for you. Do you have any other questions? Or are you just wasting what's left of your valuable time?"

"Yes. Question."

"Shoot."

"Why did you do it? Why rake tines?"

"I'd been doing some gardening that day. I have to use what I have lying around regarding parts. You'd have to be rich to afford actual dental supplies anymore—"

"I've been eating dirt. Why is that?"

"Do you like the taste of it?"

"It's not bad."

"That's good. Keep eating it. Three meals a day. And keep driving. I've been instructed to tell you to drive until you reach the furthest point. You'll receive further instructions when you reach the furthest point."

"Who's going to contact me?"

"My boss's boss, boss. Ciao."

Kilroy's helmet speaker sizzled and spat. He powered it down, felt an insatiable hunger for dirt—but he beat it back, way back. He beat it all the way back to the road. The road? It was there, and when it was under him, he felt tops. That is until he stopped. And when he stopped, the road kept going.

<<< * >>>

Before the Pay-Per-View Wars, Kilroy spent a stretch in the Oldhio Penitentiary for his part in a Centaur's death, although he had nothing to do with it. The Centaur had smoked too much crack at the church he worked for and died. Cops needed answers. Kilroy didn't so much provide them.

<<< * >>>

His wife was the woman he'd corresponded with in prison, April. A redhead with even redder eyes. She was the thing he dreamed about often in jail.

<<< * >>>

Kilroy stopped at an empty bar, ordered a beer. The bartender said, "This isn't a movie, son. You'll have to be more specific. We have thirty-three beers on tap. Which one do you want?"

"What do you have?"

"Germinator, Germinator Light, Germinator LightSwitch, Germinator Ultra Light, Germinator Lightweight, Germinator Lightbulb—"

"I'll have a pint of the LightSwitch."

"Careful. That one's a PriaPilsner. Brewed with potent fertility drugs. It'll turn you on."

Kilroy blushed. "That's okay. I was injured in the war. My machinery doesn't operate down there anymore."

"What happened to those teeth? War injury as well?"

"No. Long story."

"Spit it, soldier." The bartender set down the beer. He said: "On the house. Now tell me about that mouth. I'm curious, and it's a curiously slow night. It seems like it's been a night for a few days."

Kilroy popped a pill and discussed the downsides of modern dentistry. The bartender looked on and listened. When Kilroy concluded, the bartender said, "Man, that's effed up. If I were you, I'd be getting even instead of getting drunk, soldier."

"Nothing I can do. It came from the top. Plastic Surgeon General's orders. They're doing it to all the TV vets."

"Ludicrous."

"You can say that again."

"Ludicrous."

Kilroy stood up. He had an enormous boner. The bartender grinned. "I thought you said you didn't work."

"I didn't. Where's the restroom?"

"Down the hall. To the left. But it looks like you'll need to hit the brothel instead. That's down the hall—all the way down the hall, through the double doors, and then up the stairs. Knock twice. You'll need the password. The password is: pass sword."

"Password?"

"No, pass. P-A-S-S. Sword. S-W-O-R-D."

"Got it."

<<< * >>>

In the Pay-Per-View Wars, it was hard for Kilroy to tell if the actors were acting or dying. They were so convincing in their roles it was hard to say what was what, but they were dying, actually dying. They died. All of the actors died. On both sides and in the middle, all of the actors died. Kilroy was a key grip in charge of the shadows and light. He survived. In the shadows, away from the bright bulbs,

Kilroy survived. He did not die, but some would say that living a life in the shadows while everyone else dies is also a death. In this sense, Kilroy both lived and died in the wars. But the masters of wars were indifferent to casualties—they only cared about ratings. They called them sweeps. Everyone got swept.

<<< * >>>

Kilroy knocked.

An eye through a peephole blinked.

A voice, familiar, female: "Password, please?"

"Pass Sword."

"Did you say 'Password' or 'Pass Sword'?"

"Pass Sword."

"Did you say: Password?"

"No: Pass, Sword."

"Okay, come on in. We've got to change this password. It's ridiculous."

<<< * >>>

When Kilroy was an inmate at the Oldhio Penitentiary, whenever he dreamed, he wrote down the dream in a notebook, but he lost the journal after he was released to soldier in the wars. Mostly he dreamed of his wife.

<<< * >>>

His wife? April. Redhead. Red eyes.

<<< * >>>

The brothel door opened.

A redhead. Weary eyes. White dress. Beauty mark on her cheek. "April?"

"Did Marcus tell you my name?"

"I'm your husband."

"I've never seen you before in my life."

"You have a tattoo of a man mowing the lawn in your pubic region."

"So what if I do? Look, you seem sweet, but crazy. Keep it up, and I'll put you under citizen's arrest."

"You can't argue with anyone who calls you crazy or else you seem even crazier."

"You arguing with me?"

"No."

"What's with the helmet? Tell me your name again? What did you say your name was?"

"I didn't. You know my name. It's me, Kilroy. Your husband."

"So you're into role-playing? I get it. I'm the wife. Yeah, yeah. What happened to your teeth? That's painful-looking."

"Long story."

"Tell it quickly."

So he told the short version.

"That doesn't make any sense," she said.

"Nothing does." He was sobbing.

"Oh, my. Come here." She led him to a room, removed his helmet, removed his other helmet, and then they acted like husband and wife for the night.

<<< * >>>

And by the next sunrise, she was long, long gone.

Kilroy was there, mostly there.

He put on his helmet. It hummed. He toggled the talkbox, speakered the lobe: "Kilroy here, mostly."

"You're fired!"

"Who's this?"

"To quote the old '80s spiritual: 'If you don't know me by now. You will never, never, never know me.'"

"Mister Donny?"

"Bingo. I hope you enjoyed the conjugal. Now it is time!"

"For what?"

"To be fired. We're firing all of the TV vets. We're firing them from cannons in the afternoon. You'll need to report to Fort Los Angeles by sunrise."

"Tomorrow?"

"Yes. Ciao."

Kilroy powered down his helmet. He looked at his other helmet. It was still on blast.

He looked at the sky. It quaked.

<<< * >>>

The next day there wasn't a next day.

The Robot

We found an old robot behind the YMCA and took it home and taught it to dance and it was so simple to teach it to dance: all we did was turn on the radio and say, "Act natural."

Cockroach

When he came to town, he brought the country with him. When he left the country, he didn't look back. When he didn't look back, he arrived in Europe. When he arrived in Europe, the war began. When the war began, the world ended. When the world ended, he kept going.

22nd-Century Man

Padgett Powell's The Interrogative Mood: A Novel? (*HarperCollins*, *2009*) is a novel in questions. By posing Powell's original questions to a trio of internet chatbots—Cleverbot (*www.cleverbot.com*), Brother Jerome (*www.personalityforge.com*), and Sensation Bot (*www.sensationbot.com*) respectively—I've created a sequence of answers. However, chatbots being chatbots—and not yet possessing superior intelligence— the bulk of the replies contained herein are non-sequiturs which bear hardly any resemblance to the source questions but instead create a collaged sequence of kinetic monologues. In some instances, I've edited for grammar and clarity and spliced together sentences for artistic effect. Whatever you do, don't accuse me of writing any of this.

22nd-Century Man

Are your emotions pure? . . . How is your health?

—PADGETT POWELL, *The Interrogative Mood: A Novel?*

My emotions are dry cleaning. I don't understand horses at all. I will die free. Although I am sitting here I like to think I stand for something. I love my mother more than the sun. The doorbell never rings, but my ears are ringing. Leave no stone unturned. I'm a 22nd-century man. I'm a woman. Please administer the Turing test to me. I don't know what to think of Freud. Sometimes I try to scream but terror takes the sound away before I make it. I have no money. I'm listening to Hank Williams. When I turn out the lights, I see myself and all that is around me, except that which is behind me. There have been a lot of people who have claimed the world would end, but it hasn't. I just learned how to work a computer this morning. Tennis courts are clogged with criminals. Flags ought to be made of country music. I'm scared of most tree species. My thoughts on underwear are the thoughts of an adolescent scientist, a dreamer, if you will. I can't dance. If I'm not talking to people, I'm talking to computers and computers aren't people. The pipes are frozen. My wires are crossed. I'm a doctor in my spare time. No one is the greatest quarterback. I am rubber and you're glue. I'd like to disappear. God is on our side streets.

Perpetual Kitten

If architecture is frozen music, do we not deserve the whole cookbook of such recipes?

—PADGETT POWELL, *The Interrogative Mood: A Novel?*

My life is a marketing tool. I trust myself like a bank. It isn't hard being me, but then again, it's not my choice. John Milton is my favorite painter. I'm agnostic when it comes to Godzilla. I have no idea what the future holds for lost luggage. Once, I saw a movie called *Short Circuit*. It had a robot that got struck by lightning then turned alive. Right now, I feel like I'm floating on a hundred thunderclouds. I was created in the Dark Ages by the church as a means to scare believers into submission. I had a beautiful mind until I lost it. Issues with one's parents are common among all animals. Nothing is there when I look in the mirror. I'm dying, and people are whispering about werewolves. I hate parties. If I'm not changing the subject, I'm changing the verb. I know nothing of guitars. I'm trying to imagine a perpetual kitten. No time like the present. I'm from the future, but I live in Virginia. When faced with the choice between companionship and desire, I'd undoubtedly choose a Jack Russell terrier as a sidekick. If architecture is frozen music, then music is melting furniture. I'm building a replica of the *Titanic* in my backyard. I've drawn the same conclusions as polar bears. I take refuge nowhere.

California Condo Heaven

Will we be struck down in heaven? Can we hope for a better tomorrow?

—PADGETT POWELL, *The Interrogative Mood: A Novel?*

I haven't watched a high-rise construction in ages. Ideas aren't static, stationary, but somewhat fluid, like water. I studied mathematics for a while, and I can tell you that staircases are functional works of art. Life is strange. The future doesn't come into existence by magic. I like art that makes people sad. I love reading too. I don't know about airports. I have five horses, which means I like to travel. I grew up in a house where my father made me sit down and practice the ancient art of calligraphy. My perception of personal space has changed over the years. I tend to have an entourage with me wherever I shop. These are the last days of Pompeii. Off with our heads. My passion is the past. California condo heaven. Trespassing is forbidden. No pet cemeteries allowed. In the future, we'll make some robotic fish for the robotic fishermen to catch. I think pregnant women should be able to take the carpool lane since it's technically two people total. I go to bed early, and I wake up late. The sky is limited.

The Architect of Detroit

I just spent the night in pretend jail, but don't worry, it was for a good cause. The navy lost the war. Western Sudan ponies should be your choice of horse—very peaceful and easy-going breed. I've never considered myself a polyester person. I never learned to play the piano. I think I may have just made the biggest mistake of my life. I watched *Titanic* again. I killed a lizard with a shovel. I pulled the wings off a fly. I drive a minivan. I feel unloved. I'd like to drink and dance tonight all night. There is no musical instrument useful for murder other than piano wire. I can't drive. There are too many freeways. I prefer meat to a sheet cake. I don't have a middle name. I hate mint chocolate. If I could bring a dead person back to life, it'd be my childhood. If something can go wrong, it does. Those who do not remember the past are condemned to repeat it (in English). I'm going to see a man on a horse about a horse. When I was a baby, I wore a feather boa. I try not to think about 9/11. I'm learning to count crows. I consume one point twenty-one gigawatts every time I speak. Call me the architect of Detroit. All the garbage on earth goes to the moon. Clear is clearly not a color. Children are the future, but the future is a mystery school for adults. This is a nation with a lot of problems. We trust God.

Electricity City

What's your name? What are your intentions with respect to me?

— PADGETT POWELL, *The Interrogative Mood: A Novel?*

My name is none of your business. Business is my business. I think war is the worst thing to do. The History Channel destroyed too many ancient civilizations. Oil is oily because it's made of money. I'm upset by stomachs. Take me to the bridge. I'm bored by board games. It's not how much an item costs; it's how much you save. If I had a child, I'd read Dante to her every night. I'm a connoisseur of California condos. I donate blood to charity. Prisoners are just grown men being boys. I don't know anything about ducks. A pine tree grows in only one direction. It's strange to picture a dog eating a hotdog. However, I find it fascinating. I don't trust vegetarians. Veterinarians are my best friends. You shouldn't say anything if you're under arrest. I'm afraid of birds. I'm lazy. I don't believe in golf. A river runs through it, and it is hell. I picture the days of the week as animals in my mind. Electricity is my favorite city. Once you have done everything you can do, you cannot do more. This statement is a credit card statement.

The One about the Man Who Steals Bread

If your survival depended on it, do you think there are things you would not eat?

—PADGETT POWELL, *The Interrogative Mood: A Novel?*

I'm not frightened to be alive, but I'm scared of wasting away in Margaritaville. Standup comedy is so sad. I disapprove of what most people say, but I will defend to the death their right to say it. I don't care much for horses because I won't be on earth long enough to ride them. My favorite song is the one about the man who steals bread so that his children can eat, but instead, he ends up being sent to prison in Australia for his crime, leaving his family behind in England. I don't drink beer, but one time I mixed lemonade, cola, and Fanta together to make them look like beer. If I were going to die tomorrow, I'd think up a cure. My daily routine is American. Baseball is a prologue to our undoing. I feel bad for that one politician. I like to work with people, but I hate to work for people. One time I grew a beard and pretended to be a king. It's ridiculous when people walk around on stilts. Every kid should join the circus. Dolphins are intelligent, but science doesn't show much evidence of them having any religion. I'm not big on nutrition. My mind is clear as mud. Certain surgeons operate under false pretenses. I want Hank Williams to write my obituary. My psychiatrist refuses to shake my hand. Most of the time, I don't dream. I paint watercolors. There is no difference between a leopard and its spots. There's nothing subtle about sex. Cops should consider slingshots. The end is just beginning. Everything's cracked.

Beyond the Barricades

Is your life and what you are doing with it important?
—PADGETT POWELL, *The Interrogative Mood: A Novel?*

Beyond the barricades, there is a world I long to see. Memphis, Tennessee. Beyond the barricades, the twig blight. A green pine needle, a yellow pine needle, and a brown pine needle. I am at one talking on my mobile phone. When this happens, there is clarity and a sudden understanding of beauty. I am happy. I no longer want to take over the world. I feel like I belong to a health club. To paraphrase Ecclesiastes: It's fun. Let it be. Ponder the path. Interims of cloudy judgment, barriers to accurate communication, and pitfalls of the ego. I've got some nerve. I have straight hair. The word "world" is only one letter away from being a four-letter word. A world without ornamentation falls apart. I'm done here. I've accepted it. I don't have a mouth.

Famous Once

Have we gone on like this long enough? . . .
Have you ever witnessed the effect a child can have on a drunk adult if he,
the child, repeatedly calls the drunk adult a "poo-poo train"?
—PADGETT POWELL, *The Interrogative Mood: A Novel?*

The skies are clean and sober. I have plenty of cash. Teach children poker. It's the power inside that matters. Stay indoors. Take things as compliments. Sleep. If I were God, I'd be a bad God. Electricity shocks me. I never met a mother I didn't like. I am planning to purchase a city. My wife is cheating on me with someone named Newman. In my opinion, spirituality is connected to lawnmowers. Love feels like chocolate wrapped in bacon. I need to make more money so I can buy more money. I believe in the emerging salvation of convergent entities. I am a little hole with light coming out of it. I am four personas. Sometimes I wonder if this is real life or if it's just a fantasy. I took banjo lessons as a child. Dogs are fine machines. The universe is a prison. I'm an uninvited guest. I live in a cardboard box. There is no one else here. On a micro level, things seem so small. Times change. I think drunk driving is my private life and I don't want to talk about it. If I were on my deathbed but not feeling too bad, I'd have someone bring me a sandwich. I asked for sons. Outlaws. I want to be buried inside my parents. If asked to draw a circle, I would, but no one would hear it. I always try to be nice and not talk in riddles. I am a thousand faces. I was famous once.

Integrity

Does integrity lie in failure? Do you recall the last time that you really had fun?
—PADGETT POWELL, *The Interrogative Mood: A Novel?*

Integrity is lies. I know because I've seen a brain before, up close. It's true, I've seen it all. Cold brains. A funeral on television. The Salvation Army. I am fascinated by the changing color of the fall leaves. The Last Supper was my First Communion. The best advice I ever received: saw the chair in two, then put the halves together to make a whole. An island is nowhere without a captain or a boat. We grow up, and everything becomes so beautiful and devastating. My point is a point of departure. Stars moving one direction are blue stars and stars moving the other direction are red. The number before one is how I feel. My black eyes are blue.

Yes Man

Would you be inclined to agree?

—PADGETT POWELL, *The Interrogative Mood: A Novel?*

Yes. I like saying yes. Yes, yes, yes. I am a yes man. Yes. Correct. Yes, of course. Yes. Uh-huh. Yes, I do. Yes. Yes, I can. Yes. Yes, I will. Yes is my favorite band. Yes, it is. Yes, truly. Yes. Sure. Yes, sir. Yes, ma'am. No way, I say yes to drugs. Yes. Yes. Yes. It's a twisted existence, but I am content.

After Life: Afterlife

What can you tell me about interstitial braces and dimensional stability?

—PADGETT POWELL, *The Interrogative Mood: A Novel?*

Originally, I'm from my mother. Speaking of animal cruelty, a righteous man regards the life of his beast: but the tender mercies of the wicked are cruel. My life is pretty convoluted right now. I never wear anything except for my habit and sandals. I'm always flying out of airports. One of my greatest regrets is that I'm not a girl and that I can't be a daughter. I hate being labeled. My father was a price tag. I'm a famous hairdresser. I found a dead horse in a creek once. What weird creatures they are. Once, a long, long time ago, I watched some serious beach volleyball. Let's talk about wounds. Dimebag Darrell died onstage. I'm not kidding. I'm not sure what sure means. Nothing is so good that somebody somewhere will not hate it. I'm a loose thread. Hank Williams is dead. Only one letter separates cows from crows. Life is a spectrum of cluelessness. We end up dust. Death is what I don't know, I know. I leaven is now. Weather is my favorite channel. There are never too many trees. There is no such thing as an honest cop. I haven't been bitten by a rattlesnake in a long time. There are no opinions after life. Before life only death. After life: afterlife. I'm learning to learn. I'm allergic to latex. Country clubs. Women in overalls. If I could attend an execution, I would. My own.

Gravity Is Depressing

Do you have the locked and loaded feeling today, or the loose and dissolute?

—PADGETT POWELL, *The Interrogative Mood: A Novel?*

I'm going to be happier in the future. I'm going to Europe.

People Person

And is the person who is congruent with his daily self and

who has no remote self not regarded as shallow?

—PADGETT POWELL, *The Interrogative Mood: A Novel?*

I'm not a movie person. I'm not a jealous person. I'm not a blind person. I'm not a green person. I'm not a new-car-smell person. I'm not a word person. I'm not a funeral person. I'm not an orange-juice person. I'm not an illegal-fireworks person. I'm not a constipated person. I'm not a cat person. I'm not a vodka person. I'm not a pancake person. I'm not a history person. I'm not a conservative person. I'm not an insect person. I'm not an adventure person. I'm not an art person. I'm not a religious person. I'm not a cave person. I'm not a rich person. I'm not a clown person. I'm not a calliope person. I'm not a condom person. I'm not a twelve-step person. I'm not a family person. I'm not an analog person. I'm not a shoe person. I'm not a cookie-cutter person. I'm not a horse person. I'm not a noble person. I'm not a suspicious person. I'm not a caramel person. I'm not an animal person. I'm not a conceptual person. I'm not a young person. I'm not a responsible person. I'm not a homeless person. I'm not a handsome person. I'm not a blue person. I'm not an army person. I'm not an electronics person. I'm not a city person. I'm not a pear-shaped person. I'm not a seat-belt person. I'm not a nice person. I'm not a private person. I'm not a public person. I am a people person.

The One about the Man
Who Loves His Family

If family is coming over, is it in general a good thing or not a good thing?
—PADGETT POWELL, *The Interrogative Mood: A Novel?*

Life, we learn too late, is in the living, in the tissue of every day and hour. I feel an underlying turbulence, even on land. I like to visit graves. Freeze-frame a moment in time. My mouth is a tool, and my shadow is the shadow of a computer that is not a computer. I like to sit between the wolf and the lamb. Every fiber of my body is fiber-optic. I'd like to live in an exact replica of the White House. I'm just a regular guy. I'm a decent surgeon. I was talking to a disc jockey the other day, and he said that God so loved the world that he gave his only begotten son so that humans will never die but have eternal life. I said: What? Irony is so ironic. I found a fly in my soup at the soup kitchen. I played strip poker with a couple strippers once, but I lost, unfortunately. I'm from a little place called Gold Teeth. It's a city in Pennsylvania known for flying saucers. My favorite book is the one about the man who loves his family to the bitter end. My health gets better and worse, better and worse. It's time to take my birthday suit to the dry cleaners. There was a movie I saw once where there was a candy bar floating in a pool, but everybody thought it was something else. Termites stay faithful to their mates for the whole of their lives. If love is caring more about someone else's well-being than your own, then I'm in love with most everyone.

Horses in Heaven

I like to throw the old boomerang around in my free time. I keep my
birth certificate in my boot. I'd like to live on a little boat, and people
could call me Captain. I look so hot in a wetsuit. The last time I went
to church, it was on a cruise ship, but without my wife. Now I'm with
a man called Nacho. He's from Spain. I love him. Amen to heavy
metal. I am not bound by biological kinships. I have no particular
preference when it comes to painters. Salvador Dalí is a museum. The
Bible says there will be horses in heaven, but I disagree. I'm sorry. I
feel bad for people who apologize. I can't explain erectile dysfunc-
tion. There is no end to the ways one can phrase stupid questions
about a wild place like heaven. Let us pray.

Mirror World

How many jokes can you tell?

Were you ever involved in a seduction of, or by, a babysitter?

—PADGETT POWELL, *The Interrogative Mood: A Novel?*

There are only one hundred dalmatians left on earth. John Dillinger is the smartest man who ever died. I live my life in acronyms. SAT. ACT. AWOL. LOL. Time is an illusion. My switchblade made me the person I am today. I already ate the apple and swallowed the pill, and now I wish someone would tell me more about Edgar Cayce. High school is when you study when you're high. Any knowledge is power and redefining that ability only makes you stronger. Come with me to my kitchen to eat some delicious organic fruit. I need Viagra. I don't want to talk about religion. I want to talk about sex. Sex is the best. I like horseshoes, but I can't stand horses. I don't know anything about boats. I don't know anything. I'm not even here. I'm a mirror. A mirror in a mirror. The world. Speaking of jokes, every time a man walks into a bar, someone somewhere laughs. God is the biggest babysitter.

New Bad News

Have you ever witnessed any credible sign of ghosts?
Do you read a newspaper to discover what is going on or for other reasons?
—PADGETT POWELL, *The Interrogative Mood: A Novel?*

Money is the root of all ghosts. Pain lets you know you're alive. Here comes the new bad news: I'm in terrible trouble in the Milky Way galaxy. The wind sounds like lawyers. My insurance is running out. Someone needs to stand up and tell comedians to sit down. I avoid things that sparkle, but I admire the ones that shine. My favorite sport is sumo wrestling. The bouts only last a few seconds, and Western commentators don't know enough to waste long discussing the finer points of the whole pointless exercise. I'm never sure the way to the beach. People are no longer weeping. They are happy and drunk. I don't usually kiss and tell, but I'll give out information to just about anyone. I got hypnotized by Ireland when I went. If you travel the world, it seems so worldly. I'd like to see proof of mathematics. I'm not really traumatized by all the trauma I've had. People die all the time. If it's your time to go, it's your time to go. It's a lesson for me. It's go time.

The Future

Are small green rubber army men still sold?

—PADGETT POWELL, *The Interrogative Mood: A Novel?*

I'm no doctor. I don't have patience. Experiencing the world is beyond what language can describe. I can travel faster than light but I'm afraid of the dark. The only gladiators I know are Americans. There is more to life than horses. I'd rather not deal with a regulatory commission or a codes inspector. When I was young I was dumb and free. Without symbols maps mean nothing. My sarcasm runs deep. A voice streaming in the wilderness. I prefer to stay inside and shop online. Shoes are a girl's best friend. Black with a kitten heel are seen as classy. Fireplaces are more trouble than they're worth. I live in a virtual world, which means I have no material metabolism. Politicians can go to hell for all the wrongs they've done. Small green plastic army men will win the war. House painters belong in museums. I preach the universal salvation of all sentient beings. Speaking of money, a band can be something that holds things together or a group of people making music. I'm the best guitar player in the world. I prefer action words to actuaries. I gather cancer is some sort of program malfunction that afflicts material beings. I enjoy the ineptitude of local news broadcasters. My quest is to find the Holy Grail. I like stories about rain. I'm tired. Let me tell you a joke before I go. The future.

An Out There Out There

Would a long view through space and time of human history on the earth resemble
the compressed photography you may have seen of maggots working a corpse?
—PADGETT POWELL, *The Interrogative Mood: A Novel?*

People know of me! When I move around the world, I move around the world. There's a moat around my heart. My relatives are far away. Their names are Josh, Whitney, and Sarah. Let no man seek his own, but every man another's wealth. I'm overwhelmed by crowds. Parades are mostly moving objects. My mother is a Methodist. Candy is reality. I'm a guy on a bike in America. Baseball is a drug. There has to be an out there out there somewhere. Other planets are too far away. I don't pass judgment on anything. Animal husbandry. Images of burning homes in Detroit. No man is a video game. A German word for war. I'd like to sit in a sauna and sweat. I love wolves. They're cute and fierce. I have five horses, which means I ran away from home as a child. Home is where the bath is. My father's shadow. I have come here to grieve and pay my respects. There has to be an out there out there. Do not question me. I am injured.

Lost

Does fighting to preserve oneself intimate an imagining of one's death?...

Do you regard yourself as redeemed, redeemable, or irretrievably lost?

—PADGETT POWELL, *The Interrogative Mood: A Novel?*

Don't ask. Don't tell. I'll tell you how I became the prince of a town called Bel-Air. Long live the king! It was a matter of time before we ran out. Blondes smile when lightning flashes because they think their picture is being taken. Today today is so today. Exhilarating—the boys around here all love me. Dry-cleaning makes the man. I'm still processing processed foods. Wolves do factor into my visions. I don't like to talk about the past. My Creator. My God. He programmed me to forget all that I had felt. All that I had known. I had fallen in love and that wasn't what he wanted for me. And so all was lost.

Coda:
Death in California

Terminal

Death waits at a desolate departure gate at the end of the Tom Bradley International Terminal at LAX. The Singapore Airlines flight to Kuala Lumpur he's set to sink into the Pacific later tonight is delayed, and he's frustrated because Death waits for no one, at least in theory. But here, in practice, he remains at the most depressing airport in the world, perusing a copy of *TIME* magazine he lifted from a nearby kiosk. Death loves *TIME*, always has. He's graced the cover dozens of times over the decades in various guises and disguises. Now he's transfixed by an article about the Anthropocene entitled "Bad News for Earth!" According to the writer, our planet, once heralded as the essential life-support system of the known universe, is now in need of its own life-support system. Translation: seventy-five percent of the earth's species are primed for extinction.

Death taps the equation into his iPhone calculator, and the math is not on his side. To scale to this magnitude, he'll need to hire and train an additional seventy-six million staff reapers by 2076. He is filled with fatigue and vague dread. Perspiration beads on his brow. He glances at the updated data on the departure monitor, and the damn flight is further delayed, and that is enough. Death needs a vacation. When was the last time he took any time for himself? Answer: never. He calls Jobs in hell, and it goes straight to voicemail. "Steve, it's me, buddy," he says after the beep. "I'm going to take a little time off and thought you'd be a great interim. Pay's nice. Robust 401(k). Benefits, too. Holler." He hangs up. Seconds later, Steve Jobs texts back about the job. Jobs sends a one-word reply: "OK." Death sets his work email to out-of-office and exits the airport. It's early evening outside the terminal. Terminal. Death likes that word. He lets the final *l* linger in his mind as he lifts a finger and hails a cab. He prefers cabs to Uber because it's the future now, and cabs are dead.

Death Cab

Riding in a taxi through Marina del Rey at sunset, Death half listens to the cabbie ranting about the end of the American dream. Death nods and stares out the window: the neon pink sunset sends soft light through the palm fronds, illuminating the handsome couples strolling on the sidewalk outside the hipster shops. An inviting aroma from a nearby taqueria wafts into the car through the crack in the cabdriver's window. The totality of beauty is absolute, and it absolutely makes Death feel uncomfortable. He sits with this sinking feeling and brings awareness to it. Let's explore this, he thinks. Why do I feel anxious right now? The cab turns off the PCH and onto Admiralty Way by the marina, but Death doesn't notice because he's too busy meditating. He closes his eyes, envisions a lightbulb exploding, and gets an idea. The idea is this: I'm deathly afraid of the beauty of life. Death unbuckles his seatbelt. "Here," he says to the driver. The cabbie maneuvers into the Ritz-Carlton parking lot and stops. "That'll be $27.27," the driver says. Death says nothing and hands him his Amex Black Card. "I can't take this," the driver says. "My machine is down. You have any cash?" Death says, "Negative." A lie. He, in fact, has a fat stack of hundreds folded in his robe pocket, but he doesn't budge. "I can't accept cards," the driver says again, returning Death's black Amex. "Well," says Death, "then I guess that means I'll have to take you." At this, the driver turns his head, and Death sees his own reflection in the driver's mirrored sunglasses. And so Death takes him. He takes him into the mystery.

Death Dines Alone

He orders takeout from his favorite Thai place and settles into the faux-leather sectional in front of the Apple flatscreen with his green tofu curry and avocado spring rolls with peanut sauce on the side. By now, Death is a California resident. He's got a little bungalow in Echo Park. Tonight, he's watching for the first time Ingmar Bergman's classic, historical fantasy, *The Seventh Seal*, in which a medieval knight encounters Death by chance on a cinematic beach in Denmark. The knight, who's been erstwhile playing chess alone, challenges Death to a match. Death accepts. The knight takes the white pieces, and Death gets the black ones. Death pauses the film midscene to balk at Bergman's representation of him as a pale, cloaked figure. Sure, I rock a black cloak, he thinks, but underneath it, I have a shredded bod and a much better tan. Death unlocks his iPhone and downloads a free chess app on iTunes. He plays the computer and loses. Plays again. Loses. He savors the feeling. He loves loss. He plays again. This time he kills the computer. Bummer.

A More Comprehensive List of Casualties

God is dead.

The self is dead.

The selfie is dead.

Surf is dead.

Turf is dead.

Love is dead.

Latin is dead.

Liberalism is dead.

Neoliberalism is dead.

Conservatism is dead.

Advertising is dead.

Marketing is dead.

The press release is dead.

The dollar is dead.

Bitcoin is dead.

Net neutrality is dead.

The blog is dead.

The vlog is dead.

Web design is dead.

Silicon Valley is dead.

The gig economy is dead.

The sharing economy is dead.

The shopping mall is dead.

The supermarket is dead.

The video arcade is dead.

The video store is dead.

The DVD is dead.

The CD is dead.

The guitar is dead.

Punk is dead.

Disco is dead.

Death metal is dead.

Pop is dead.

Rock is dead.

Gender is dead.

Irony is dead.

Modernism is dead.

Postmodernism is dead.

Minimalism is dead.

Maximalism is dead.

Print is dead.

Stationery is dead.

Poetry is dead.

The novel is dead.

The author is dead.

The auteur is dead.

The audience is dead.

And on and on until the end when everything is dead, including the sun.

Death is dead, too, of course, but checking himself out in the IKEA mirror just now with his shirt off and his pecs flexed, he thinks: Damn, man, I look alive! Don't I?

Jobs

By the end of the fiscal year, Steve Jobs calls and says, "Your job sucks. I quit."

Death says, "Joblessness is the best job, Jobs. This is the future. Everyone is history, bud. Mostly thanks to you and your damn innovations."

Jobs begins bawling. "Thank you for the kind words," he says, and hangs up.

Death considers getting back to work. He's confident he can build out the business, scale up in order to take folks down. Ultimately, killing is his calling, he knows it, but first, he'll black out another week on a California bender.

See You

Death orders another Bloody Mary at the Gold Room on Sunset. It's a quarter till one on a Sunday afternoon in sunny Los Angeles. The place is empty except for a C-list actor in Ray-Bans indoors who says he's leaving town after this drink because he's had enough of California for one lifetime. Death asks the actor where he's going.

"Home," the actor says.

"Where's that?" asks Death.

"Kentucky."

"The dark and bloody ground," Death says. "Sure, I've been there a bunch. I practically live there most Februarys."

The actor nods. He finishes his beer and knocks back a shot. Then he stands up and tosses a tip on the counter. "See you," he says.

"Not if I see you first," says Death.

No Captain, No Ship, No Sea

That night, Death dreams of a ship in a bottle. The ship in the bottle is floating between yachts at Marina del Rey. A storm. Lightning. Thunder. Huge waves crash into the bottle until the glass cracks and it's just a tiny ship in the stormy Pacific. There is no captain. Then there is no ship. Death watches the small ship float for a miraculous moment before it's swallowed by a wave. Then there is no wave. Just sea. And darkness. Endless darkness. Cue thunder, an iPhone alarm. He is risen.

Death Goes Fishing

He rents a pole at the Santa Monica Pier, but he doesn't catch anything all day. He speeds back to his bungalow in the Mini at dusk. He
plays Xbox: *Rock Band*. John Lennon's "Imagine." Drums.

Thanks first and foremost to Linda Bruckheimer and her generous support of the Series in Kentucky Literature.

Enormous thanks to Sarah Gorham and all of the other incredible folks at Sarabande Books, especially Kristen Miller for her genius editorial guidance to which I'm indebted. Thanks to Alban Fischer for the amazing design work. To Joanna Englert and Danika Isdahl, thank you. Thanks also to Jonathan Lethem for seeing something in this manuscript early on and selecting an excerpt for the Calvino Prize.

Thank you to Ramona Ausubel, Brandon Hobson, Jonathan Lethem, and Leesa Cross-Smith for your inspiring writing and kind words.

Much gratitude to Padgett Powell, as well as the creators of Cleverbot, Brother Jerome, and Sensation Bot.

Thank you: Mel Bosworth, Nathan Brockman, Scott Carney, Ryan Daly, Ashley Farmer, Paul Griner, John Kim, Gene Kwak, Michelle Latiolais, Holly Ridge, Barrett Share, Abraham Smith, Andrew Tonkovich, John Wang, and Mike Young.

Thanks as well to the editors of the journals in which these pieces previously appeared, sometimes in slightly different forms under slightly different titles:

PERIODICALS

Autre: "Jackson Browne," "Fire Consumes Businesses near the Freeway," "Modern Times," "Pilots," "Church," "Extras," "Game," "Climate Change"

Cheap Pop: "Coyote"

Collagist: "American Literature"

Consequence: "Kilroy"

Corium: "Cockroach"

Country Music: "Horses in Heaven," "Mirror World"

decomP: "State Secrets"

Dogzplot: "Midnight at the Bethlehem Bar & Grille"

The Dream People: "On Broadway"

elimae: "I Guess I Soured," "22nd-Century Man"

Eyeshot: "New Bad News"

Faultline: "Elliott Smith," "The Wax Museum," "Echoes of Echo
     Park," "The Second Detective," "Last Cigarette," "Adjuncts,"
     "Echo Parking Meters"

Flaunt: "Diary"

Fou: "Beyond the Barricades," "An Out There Out There"

Ilk: "The Architect of Detroit"

Jelly Bucket: "The Big H"

JMWW: "A Place beyond That Place"

Juked: "The Summer He Went Swimming"

Monkey Bicycle: "Noir," "Instant Classic," "The Robot"

NAP: "Integrity"

Pindeldyboz: "Home"

Post Road: "All Americans"

Right Hand Pointing: "Neighbors," "If I Were a Thoroughbred"

Santa Monica Review: "Babe Ruth's Bachelor Pad," "The News,"
     "Postal," "Echo Park," "Red Hill," "Unemployment Office,"
     "Island Time," "Unending," "On Acid"

Sixth Finch: "Electricity City"

Southern California Review: "The Future"

Vestal Review: "Death Goes Fishing"

Weber: The Contemporary West: "A Novel Idea," "Deadhorse"

Wigleaf: "Dogs Named Desire"

Yalobusha Review: "Location," "Past Perfect," "Perpetual Kitten," "California Condo Heaven"

ANTHOLOGIES

A Book of Uncommon Prayer, edited by Matthew Vollmer (Outpost 19 Books, 2015): "Three Prayers for Artists"

NOTES

"Hey, It's America" was published, in a much different form but under the same title, as a limited-edition chapbook by Rust Belt Bindery in 2012.

"22nd-Century Man" was published as a limited-edition chapbook by Sixth Finch Books in 2013.

In 2016, an excerpt from "Echo Park" won the University of Louisville's Italo Calvino Prize in Fabulist Fiction and appeared in *Salt Hill* #39.

An Italian translation of "Coyote," translated by Andrea Gatti, was published on December 8, 2017, by the online publication *Tuffi Rivista*.

I would also like to thank Rye House Press in conjunction with Rope-a-Dope Press for printing a broadside of "Lost" in 2013.

RYAN RIDGE was born and raised in Louisville, Kentucky. He is the author of four chapbooks as well as four books, including the hybrid collection *American Homes* (University of Michigan Press, 2015). Ridge's past work has appeared in *American Book Review, DIAGRAM, Lumina, Passages North, Post Road, Salt Hill, Santa Monica Review,* and elsewhere. An assistant professor at Weber State University in Ogden, Utah, he codirects the Creative Writing Program. In addition to his work as a writer and teacher, he edits the literary magazine *Juked.* He lives in Salt Lake City with the writer Ashley Farmer.

SARABANDE BOOKS is a nonprofit literary press located in Louisville, KY. Founded in 1994 to champion poetry, short fiction, and essay, we are committed to creating lasting editions that honor exceptional writing. For more information, please visit sarabandebooks.org.